W9-CKV-853

The Memory of Forgotten Things

Also by Kat Zhang

The Emperor's Riddle

The Memory of Forgotten Things

KAT ZHANG

Aladdin

NEW YORK LONDON TORONTO SYDNEY NEW DELHI

J

This book is a work of fiction. Any references to historical events, real people, or real places are used fictitiously. Other names, characters, places, and events are products of the author's imagination, and any resemblance to actual events or places or persons, living or dead, is entirely coincidental.

ALADDIN
An imprint of Simon & Schuster Children's Publishing Division
1230 Avenue of the Americas, New York, New York 10020
First Aladdin hardcover edition May 2018
Text copyright © 2018 by Cathy Zhang
Jacket illustration copyright © 2018 by Jim Tierney
ALADDIN and related logo are registered trademarks of Simon & Schuster, Inc.
For information about special discounts for bulk purchases,
please contact Simon & Schuster Special Sales at 1-866-506-1949
or business@simonandschuster.com.
The Simon & Schuster Speakers Bureau can bring authors to your live event. For more information or to book an event contact the Simon & Schuster Speakers Bureau at 1-866-248-3049 or visit our website at www.simonspeakers.com.
Jacket designed by Jessica Handelman
Interior designed by Tom Daly
The text of this book was set in Weiss Std.
Manufactured in the United States of America 0418 FFG
2 4 6 8 10 9 7 5 3 1
Library of Congress Cataloging-in-Publication Data
Names: Zhang, Kat, author.
Title: The memory of forgotten things / by Kat Zhang.
Description: First Aladdin hardcover edition. |
New York : Simon Pulse, 2018. | Summary: "Twelve-year-old Sophia has never told anyone about her unusual memories—snapshots of a past that never happened. She becomes convinced that the upcoming solar eclipse will grant her the opportunity to make her alternate life come true, to enter a world where her mother never died. With the help of two misfit boys, she must figure out a way to bring her mother back to her— before the opportunity is lost forever"— Provided by publisher.
Identifiers: LCCN 2017039499 |
ISBN 9781481478656 (hc) | ISBN 9781481478670 (eBook)
Subjects: | CYAC: Mothers—Fiction. | Grief—Fiction. | Memory—Fiction.
Classification: LCC PZ7.Z454 Me 2018 | DDC [Fic]—dc23
LC record available at https://lccn.loc.gov/2017039499

For Savannah,
who taught me so much when I was just
beginning, and who is always the first to read

The Memory of Forgotten Things

1

THE MEMORY STRUCK SOPHIA MUCH LIKE the others.

It was just before first bell at Jessup Middle School. Kids swarmed around her—streaming off school buses, jumping out of minivans, cruising up on their hand-me-down bikes.

An indecently red car screeched to the curb, throwing a hush over the morning bustle. Everyone knew that car. It belonged to Nicole Johnson, who'd bought it months ago after her sixteenth birthday. It hadn't been much at first—a skeleton car rolling on bald wheels, coated in a bygone dream of glamour. Nicole had bribed and cajoled (and blackmailed, people whispered) the local auto shop until she'd transformed that clunker into a gleaming beast.

She roared through town on it every morning, pausing on her way to Holden High to drop off her little brother, DeAndre.

And every morning the kids of Jessup Middle stopped to stare. Their town was a town of pickups and minivans and practical old cars with more mileage on them than paint. It was not the sort of town one roared through in a red convertible, even if it was patched together and secondhand.

Nicole didn't care. She perched like a queen in the driver's seat, adjusting her cloud of black curls while DeAndre—DJ—slipped from the car. He mumbled something, but Sophia didn't catch the words.

Because right then, the Memory hit her.

The world jolted. Sophia's stomach flipped like it did at the top of a roller coaster. Only there was no fall—just a shudder that shocked her from chest to fingertips.

The Memory didn't take her away from Jessup. She still stood at the back of the school, a few yards from the door. She heard the bus monitors telling everyone

Good morning, heard slamming car doors and rumbling bus engines. The air shimmered with the tang of rusty metal and hot asphalt.

She held something in her hands—a lunch box. Which was weird, because Sophia never packed lunch. Not when she got it for free at school.

But in the Memory, the lunch box in her hands was blue and purple, her two favorite colors. She shifted it to one hand so she could wave with the other.

Bye! she shouted.

Good-bye! someone shouted back. A woman in the carpool lane with Sophia's straight brown hair and dark, deep-set eyes.

The Memory ended. Sophia tumbled back to the here and now. To the lunch-box-less emptiness in her hands.

None of the other students had noticed anything. They shoved past Sophia, lost in their chattering and laughter as they headed inside.

No, that wasn't true. Someone had noticed.

DJ watched her, intent to the point of staring. Probably wondering what on earth was wrong with her.

Sophia forced her legs moving again. Hurried

inside, her book bag bouncing against her back.

And tenderly, in the back of her mind, she filed this new Memory away with the others.

Like everyone, Sophia had a lifetime of memories. In her case, a lifetime was a little under thirteen years. Some parts of it, of course, stood out more than others. The time she'd broken her wrist in third grade. The first-grade chorus concert when she'd sung a solo.

But nearly all of Sophia's happiest memories, the really special ones, involved her mother.

Like the memory of her tenth birthday, when her mother made her a cake from scratch. Sophia remembered the way the frosting tasted, the way the pink sugar roses dissolved on her tongue.

She remembered, too, the tiny nativity scene she and her mother built together when Sophia was seven. The time they went to the town festival when she was nine.

These memories were all Sophia had of her mother, so she kept them close—shuffled through them like old photographs, half-frightened that too much handling would do damage.

She kept them secret, too. Because as paltry as these memories were, she shouldn't have had them at all.

Sophia's mother had died when she was six years old. But that wasn't how she remembered it.

Not always.

2

SCHOOL DAYS NEVER FELT AS LONG AS they did in May. Heat baked the blacktops. Jessup's ancient air conditioners wheezed lukewarm air while children sat melting in their plastic seats. This particular Wednesday dragged along even slower than most. By the time Sophia reached her final block with Mr. Rae, she was pretty sure the sun would explode before last bell.

The rest of her class agreed. Mr. Rae spent the block telling people to *Please turn around in your seat*, to *Stop talking*, to *Take your head off your desk—this isn't nap time*. But getting the seventh-grade class to behave was like taming a river.

As soon as Mr. Rae said, "All right, that's enough poetry for today. Give me a minute to return your critical essays," the room tumbled into chaos.

"It's almost the end of the year." Mr. Rae raised his voice to be heard over the clamor. "Just one more project before you're free for the summer."

The kids still paying attention groaned. Most were too engrossed in their conversations to care. In the middle of the fuss, Sophia's desk was a quiet island. She closed her eyes, rested her knobby elbows on her desk, and sank back into the Memory from this morning.

A *Memory* was different from normal memories. Sometimes they came late at night, while she lay half-asleep in bed. Sometimes they came while she walked home from school, choked by roadside dust and afternoon humidity. Sometimes, like this one, they came in the morning.

Always, they hit like a semitruck.

If a regular memory was like dipping a toe in a puddle, a Memory was like being tossed into the Pacific Ocean. From a helicopter.

Capital *M* Memories transported her to . . . Somewhere Else. They made her dream while awake.

Once a Memory struck her, it lingered like a normal one. But that meant it could fade like a normal memory too. Sophia was trying to solidify the Memory of her mother's smile—her wave good-bye—when the sound of her name startled everything away.

"What?" She blinked and looked up.

Mr. Rae smiled as he set her essay on her desk. He was a giant of a man, and when he waved his hands around as he talked—which he always did—he seemed even bigger. The seventh-grade classroom, with its crowded desk space and scant line of windows, was barely large enough to contain him.

Mr. Rae should have been a gym teacher, Sophia thought. Or maybe an athlete. Perhaps a mountain climber. But in the end, she was glad he was her language arts teacher. His energy seeped into every book they read.

"You're in a group with DJ and Luke," he said. "For the project."

"Oh." She tried not to sound disappointed.

Luke McPherson wasn't in class today—it was his last day of in-school suspension. He'd gotten into an argument with a teacher. Or maybe it was an administrator. With Luke, it was always something or another. The other kids kept gleeful records of all the things he got in trouble for, but Sophia had long stopped caring.

And DJ—

She glanced at his desk, kitty-corner from her own. It was another quiet spot in the room. Nobody talked much to DJ, but he never seemed to mind. He was usually too busy reading to notice.

Right now, he had a book half-hidden in his lap. Not a regular book—a sketchbook. It looked fancy, with a thick black cover and his full name embossed in the corner: DEANDRE JAY JOHNSON.

Sophia wished she'd gotten into a group with Madison Butchner again. Or maybe Emily Dens. Both girls had been friendly when they'd worked with Sophia on previous projects. They'd invited her to their houses, let her pet their dogs and sit at their picture-perfect kitchen tables. Emily had even told her to stay for dinner, and afterward, they'd watched the second half of a movie on TV.

Neither girl had bothered talking to Sophia after their projects ended, but she didn't blame them. She hadn't tried talking to them, either.

They had friends already. They didn't need more.

Sophia wasn't sure how she'd gotten to be the way

she was—the forgotten girl in class, the one who sat alone at the edges of lunch tables, who nobody ever said hello to in the halls. She suspected it had started in first grade, when she'd suddenly become That Girl with the Dead Mom, and none of the other kids had known what to do.

In the years since then, Sophia had never shaken the label. Never managed to overcome that initial deficit.

But group projects let her pretend she was the sort of girl who got invited to people's houses.

Unless, of course, she got lumped together with the other misfits in class.

DJ glanced up and met her eyes. He snapped the sketchbook shut, but Sophia caught a glimpse of his drawing: a pencil portrait of a man with his black hair in twists. He bore a small, quirked grin. Someone DJ knew?

DJ shoved the notebook under his essay. Mr. Rae was several rows over now, so Sophia leaned over and admitted, "I didn't hear anything he said about our project."

"We're doing research papers on myths." DJ didn't sound particularly friendly or unfriendly. He held her gaze with a steadiness that was almost uncomfortable. Sophia thought about the shiny car his sister drove, thought about the creamy white paper of his sketch-book, and felt suddenly shy. "Our topic's solar eclipses."

"Thanks," Sophia said.

DJ smiled. It loosened something about him, made his eyes soften. Surprised, Sophia smiled back.

They sat like that a touch too long, silent and smiling and searching for something to say.

"There's going to be one in a little more than a week," DJ ventured. "A solar eclipse. We'll be able to see it from here."

Sophia nodded. The local news had been going on about the eclipse for ages. And even if she'd managed to miss hearing about it on TV, she couldn't have missed the display Mr. Rae had posted in his LEARN AROUND TOWN bulletin board.

"We're right in the path of totality," Sophia said. *Totality* meant the period when the moon fully shielded the sun and the world fell dark. She didn't explain this to DJ; he seemed like the kind of person who'd already know.

If anything, he seemed pleased by the fact that *she* knew. He leaned across his desk, and she followed suit. It wasn't necessary to keep their voices down—the rest of their class operated at a low roar—but Sophia liked it. It was like they were sharing secrets.

"It's been three hundred years since the last time you could see a full solar eclipse from this town," DJ said.

Sophia almost added that it had been twelve years and eleven months since the last partial eclipse, but kept quiet at the last minute.

If she spoke up, DJ might wonder how she knew. And then she'd have to tell him that she knew because she'd been born that day, right as the sky turned dusky and the world plunged into twilight.

That was too much to share. Sophia was a private sort of girl, and her walls served her well.

Once silence crept in between her and DJ, it seemed impossible to drive it away again. She fidgeted with her hair. DJ tapped his pencil eraser against his desk. Vaguely, she heard Mr. Rae telling everyone to get into their groups and decide which myth they were going to present.

What sort of eclipse myths do you know? Sophia was about to say, when there came a commotion by the door.

Luke wandered into the classroom like a lost traveler—like it was only chance and planetary alignment that had made him end up here, and not the cafeteria, or the music room, or Mars. He came in with his shoulders hunched, which was how he always walked when he wasn't angry and trying to pick a fight. Mr. Rae waved him to his desk.

DJ watched them too. Sophia waited for him to say, *I heard he got in trouble for—* But he didn't, just met her eyes meaningfully. Neither of them expected Luke to be an easy person to work with.

Mr. Rae gestured toward DJ and Sophia, who both quickly pretended like they hadn't been staring.

By the time Sophia looked up again, Luke was slouched a foot or two from her and DJ, creating the brooding third point of a quiet triangle. It was almost summer, but Luke was ghostly pale beneath his freckles.

As the seconds wore on, it became obvious that he intended to stay as silent as a ghost too.

"What sort of eclipse myths do you know?" Sophia asked.

Luke said nothing. DJ cleared his throat and offered a few ideas: cultural stories about animals swallowing the sun, a few legends about evil demons, something about solar eclipses and fasting. . . .

Sophia tried to look busy writing everything down. Luke loomed silently over the proceedings.

Only ten minutes left until afternoon announcements, Sophia told herself, and sighed. She could make it that long.

3

ON WEDNESDAYS, SOPHIA'S FATHER worked breakfast and lunch shifts at Tom's Diner, then nights at a law office in the city, mopping floors and emptying trash cans after the lawyers went home. That meant he usually had some time free in the afternoon.

Sophia came home to find him reclined on their lumpy gray couch. She studied him the way she always studied him—took in the tired smile on his face, the slump of his shoulders, the fact that he'd made himself a sandwich instead of scrounging for chips. Studying her dad was reflex now, even if things were better than they'd been for years.

The TV flashed snippets of local news: a car accident

at Willow and Maxwell, an interview with the oldest woman in town celebrating her ninety-ninth birthday.

Her dad waved her over to join him on the couch. "How was school?"

She shrugged and stole a piece of his sandwich. "We have a big project in language arts."

"Another one?" he said. "Didn't you guys just turn in an essay?"

"Mr. Rae is a big fan of projects. I'm in a group with DJ and Luke."

Her dad frowned. "Luke McPherson? That kid whose sister died?"

Everyone in town remembered when Luke's big sister had died in a car crash three years ago. And everyone at school remembered the day Luke had come back to class. How he'd flown into a rage and trashed the elementary school art room before breaking down sobbing. He'd had to be sent home.

Sophia felt a twinge of irritation. She knew her dad didn't mean anything by it, but Luke hadn't chosen to be The Boy with the Dead Sister any more than she'd chosen to be That Girl with the Dead Mom.

"Yeah, that Luke," she said.

"He still making trouble all the time?"

"I guess."

Her dad looked like he was going to add something, then changed his mind. "So what's this new project about?"

"Solar eclipses," Sophia said. "Did you know the one coming up is going to be the first one this town's seen in three hundred years?"

Her dad raised his eyebrows. "I did not know that. But I *do* know that—"

"That the last partial eclipse was almost thirteen years ago." Sophia rolled her eyes and smiled. "I haven't forgotten."

Her father laughed. Sophia loved it when she made her father laugh. His eyes crinkled, and his whole body relaxed.

He laid his hand on Sophia's head. He'd done that all the time when Sophia was younger—not ruffling her hair, just resting his palm atop her head. She was older now, but it still made her feel small and loved.

"Your mom used to say that it was only a partial eclipse because even the sun didn't want to miss your birth."

Sophia knew this tale by heart—the story that had felt too private, too precious, to share with DJ. It was one of the few stories about her mother that her father was willing to reveal. One of the few times he spoke of her at all.

She could listen to it a thousand times. A million times.

"We waited so long for you to come," her dad said. "We stayed hours and hours in the hospital. Your mom kept going on about how late you were and how the eclipse was bad luck. She was always superstitious like that. Anyway, fifteen hours into the whole thing, she suddenly got really calm. Just peaceful and happy."

Sophia's dad looked peaceful and happy now, as he told the story. If Sophia hadn't been afraid that moving might break the moment, she would have hugged him the way she'd done when she was a little girl, her head tucked against his chest.

"She told me she'd had a vision. That she'd already seen our baby girl being born, and that she was beautiful and perfect." He tugged gently at Sophia's hair. "Then out you came an hour later. And you were."

* * *

Sophia lived too close to Jessup to ride the bus, and her father often left for work before she woke, so most school days found her walking alone to school. She didn't mind. She was accustomed to it. Usually she passed the time flipping through old Memories of her mother, making sure she didn't forget the details.

For other children, who had thousands of memories of their mothers, it didn't matter if they lost a few. If they forgot what color dress she'd worn one random Thursday morning the year they were nine.

Sophia understood. Once upon a time, before her mother had fallen ill, she hadn't appreciated the moments they spent together either. They'd been plentiful, and so she'd wasted them, certain that more would come.

Now, all she had was the past. The past and the Memories, which were not truly Past, and not truly Present, but some strangeness she'd been gifted.

She was so lost in her thoughts that when she ran into DJ, she literally crashed into him. They tumbled to the ground. Sophia hadn't been holding anything, but DJ's books went flying.

"Sorry, sorry," she said, scrambling to help him pick them up. Her book bag banged against her back, throwing her off balance. She felt oddly clumsy. More flustered than she should have been. "I didn't know you walked to school—"

Your sister's always dropping you off, she thought, but she remembered the way DJ had slunk out of Nicole's car, and didn't say it.

"Nicole woke up late today." DJ shrugged and didn't meet her eyes. "I don't mind walking."

The town had decided long ago that, considering their father's antics, the Johnson kids should strive to be as respectable as possible. As if that would make up for it.

Nicole's convertible was not respectable. It was not meek. It was not at all ashamed.

The town hated it. And DJ, it seemed, was fully aware.

Sophia reached for his sketchbook, which lay splayed open on the sidewalk. A passing car made the pages ruffle. DJ was good—really good. Sophia recognized a drawing of Nicole, glimpsed a sketch of a shaggy-haired dog.

But more than anything else, there was that man again.

DJ had drawn him in portraits: staring out of the page, grinning, thoughtful. In motion: flipping a pancake at the stove, catching a football, wrestling with the dog. In repose: frowning as he thumbed through a book. Dozens and dozens of sketches of the same man, crammed ten or fifteen to a page. Some were more detailed than others. All were lovingly rendered, the lines sure and bold.

Silently Sophia handed DJ the sketchbook. Theirs was the sort of town where everybody knew everybody and it was impossible not to know everyone else's business, so she knew that DJ's dad had left when he was a baby.

Not just left, but run off so spectacularly, so awfully, that it had been top town gossip for months. Sophia had been far too young to remember it happening, but she'd heard the stories. The kids at school, the parents in the drop-off lane—everyone had heard the stories. They whispered retellings of it every morning when Nicole's convertible roared up to school.

"It's not him." DJ's fingers closed around the sketchbook. He sounded defensive, his shoulders up. "It's not my dad, I mean."

"Oh," Sophia said. "Okay. Who is it?"

The question only made DJ look even more uncomfortable, which wasn't what Sophia had meant to do at all. She didn't know how to undo it.

They stared at each other. Looked away. Met eyes again.

Sophia cleared her throat and tried to change the topic. "Did you do anything for the project? For Mr. Rae, I mean."

"A little," he said. "We should figure out how we're going to narrow things down. We can't cover it all."

They started walking again. It was strange but nice to have someone to talk to before school, Sophia decided. And DJ was different from what she'd expected too. Relaxed. Almost chatty.

Soon they'd almost reached school. DJ was telling her about the Pomo indigenous people, who told stories of a bear who fought with the sun and chomped a bite out of it.

"That's actually their phrase for 'solar eclip—'" he said, and then he went very quiet, and very still. His eyes unfocused.

He looked like he'd fallen asleep with his eyes open.

He looked like his mind was a million miles away.

He looked, Sophia thought, the way she must look when she was hit by a Memory.

4

A MOMENT LATER, DJ SHOOK OFF HIS daze. He resurfaced like a deep-sea diver, with a gasp and a wince at the sudden loudness of the world.

Sophia should have said, *Are you okay?* Should have said, *What happened?* Or *Something wrong?*

Instead she blurted out, "Do you have them too?"

"Have what?" DJ said, too quickly.

Sophia blocked his way so he couldn't keep walking. "What happened just now? What did you see?"

Sophia's father complained sometimes that she was as stubborn as a king's will. As far as Sophia was concerned, there were times when yielding was nice and polite, and there were times when you had to keep pushing until the job was done.

The fierceness of her questions caught DJ off guard. His eyebrows drew together. His chin lifted.

"What did you see yesterday morning?" he countered. "Before school. By the drop-off lane."

Now he was the one daring her to answer. Sophia's lips zipped tight.

Once, not long after her mother's death, she'd mentioned her Memories to her father. He'd told her she was imagining things. Then he'd gone quietly to his room, turned off the lights, and spent three days staring silently at the ceiling. Sophia had never told anyone about the Memories again.

They were not, she'd realized, something everyone had.

Except here was DJ with his sudden, strange touchiness. His probing question. His secretiveness about the drawings in his notebook.

Here, Sophia thought, was the time to use a king's will.

"I had a Memory." She put an emphasis, ever so slightly, on the last word, and stared DJ straight in the eyes as she said it. She hoped that was enough to hint that she didn't mean any *ordinary* memory.

"A memory? Like, you remembered something you'd forgotten?"

Sophia huffed in frustration. "No, not like that at all."

She warred with herself. If she told DJ the truth, and he blabbed about it to other people, no one would believe him. No one at school would care what DJ said about her. It was a mean sort of thought, but true. He was as invisible to their classmates as she was.

And Sophia wanted so badly to share this with someone. Telling DJ would be revealing the most vulnerable, secret side of herself. But letting this opportunity go might be even worse.

What if she was right, and DJ had the Memories too?

What if she wasn't crazy, wasn't just making them up?

"Not something that I've forgotten," she said slowly. "Something that never happened at all."

DJ regarded her warily, like he was trying to decide if she was messing with him. He didn't say, *That's impossible*, or *You're crazy*. He didn't walk away.

Sophia looked down at the pockmarked sidewalk. Then away to the line of trees by the road. And finally, back to DJ.

"I started getting them after my mom died," she

whispered. "When I was six. In the beginning, they were just flashes of something. Like the world was glitching."

She bit her lip. She wasn't explaining this right.

"The flashes started getting longer. I'd get little scenes: me and my mom at the park. Or me and my mom making dinner. They were like memories, only they'd never actually happened."

She told DJ how the Memories used to come once every few months—but now they came weekly, sometimes daily. How they were getting longer, more involved.

How they always centered around her mother.

Once she started talking about it, it was hard to stop. Only a posse of sixth graders, giggling and shouting as they crossed the street, broke her off. She took a deep breath and waited for DJ's reply.

He motioned for her to sit next to him at the edge of the sidewalk. The dry grass scratched at Sophia's legs and tickled her knees. So did the velvety cover of DJ's sketchbook when he lay it open on her lap.

She looked at him questioningly, and he nodded for her to flip through the sketchbook. So she did, taking her time now as she went through each drawing. The mystery man filled more than half the pages.

"I think he might be my stepdad," DJ said, after a long while. "I think—I think he and my mom got married a few years ago. Or should have. Or something. I don't know. I think I—well, I think I *Remember* the wedding."

This time, he emphasized *Remember* the way Sophia had emphasized *Memory*.

His smile was wistful, faint. "But I don't know. I've never met him."

5

SOPHIA MIGHT AS WELL HAVE TELEPORTED
the rest of the way to school, because she didn't remember any of it—only the way she and DJ spent the whole time talking about their Memories. It was like they'd been parched their whole lives and hadn't realized until they were finally allowed to drink.

They were so engrossed, so lost in their shared excitement, that they ignored the first morning bell. DJ was in the middle of a story about his stepfather taking him bird watching. He described his Memories with the same reverent detail that he drew his portraits, looping Sophia in so well that she could feel the brisk cold of that weekend morning, hear the quiet murmuring of the waking woods, see the flash of the birds' feathers. The second bell rang, obnoxious and prodding. They parted reluctantly, unsure how to say goodbye.

Sophia fidgeted through the rest of the day. Waiting for Mr. Rae's class—the only class she had with DJ—was torture. She was in such a rush to get to the language arts classroom that she was the first one there.

No, not the first one. She skidded through the door and almost overlooked the dark-clothed lump huddled in the back of the room. Said lump raised its head at her entrance. Its jacket hood fell back, revealing a shock of blond hair.

Luke.

He gave her a dead-eyed look, then put his head back onto his desk.

"Hello, Sophia," Mr. Rae said cheerfully.

"Hello." Sophia's eyes darted to Luke again. When they returned to Mr. Rae, he raised his eyebrows at her expectantly.

Sophia was hardly the friendliest person in class. If Mr. Rae wanted someone to coax Luke into a conversation, or bring him out of his eternal bad mood, he'd chosen the wrong girl. Sophia had always made a point of staying out of Luke McPherson's way, and he'd returned the favor.

She lingered by the doorway, waiting to see if someone else might come through. No luck. Everyone stood chatting by their lockers.

And she was in here. With Luke.

"Go ahead and sit with your project groups today," Mr. Rae said, nudging.

Sophia sidled up to Luke's desk and cleared her throat.

It took a few seconds, but he lifted his head again. They stared at each other. Then, with a sigh like all this—Sophia, the assignment, being alive right now in the grinding almost-summer heat—was the biggest inconvenience in the world, Luke sat up.

Sophia sat at the desk in front of his and turned so they faced each other. She thought about saying something, but everything sounded stupid, even in her head. Besides, he looked so sulky and obstinately disagreeable that she didn't want to talk with him at all.

Luke McPherson was a minefield, and Sophia liked her limbs intact.

They sat in silence, holding eye contact. Luke was the first to blink and look away.

"I don't know anything about solar eclipses." He said it like a challenge.

Sophia shrugged.

Where was DJ? Had he been waiting all day to see her, the way she'd been waiting to see him? Her stomach couldn't settle until they spoke again—until she could be sure he wasn't going to show up and say, *Actually, I was just kidding about everything this morning.*

The other kids filed in, their presence defusing some of the tension in the room. DJ took the desk beside Sophia's. He smiled at her, and her lungs loosened.

If Luke noticed the look between them, he ignored it.

"All right," Mr. Rae said once everyone was seated. "We're headed to the library today so you can start gathering sources for your project."

Sophia slipped next to DJ as they spilled into the hall. Their classmates jostled them close to each other.

"I have something to tell you," she whispered.

"About the project?"

"About the Memories." She paused to organize her thoughts. "When I was born, my mom—I think she had a Memory too. She had these visions of me *already* being born. Like she'd already been through it before it actually happened. That could mean something, don't you think?"

DJ frowned. "Was that the only time? You think it's genetic or something?"

"Maybe?" Sophia said. "I guess it could be unrelated, but I don't know. I was born during the partial eclipse, and my mom—"

"Wait, wait," DJ said. "You were born during the partial eclipse? On June—"

"June eleventh," Sophia said. "Yes, that's right. Why?"

He grinned at her. He had a really great grin, the kind that lit up his eyes and traveled through his whole body. "That's my birthday too."

Sophia was startled quiet. She and DJ had gone to school together for years, yet she'd never registered that they shared a birthday. She supposed she'd never known DJ enough to care. She'd just known *of* him, and figured it was enough.

She looked at him—really looked, and paid attention.

Unlike Luke, DJ hadn't hit his growth spurt yet; he was only an inch or two taller than Sophia. His dark brown legs were nearly as skinny as her own—and Sophia, her father teased, was nothing but knees and elbows. Unlike Sophia, he had a burgeoning sense of fashion: a collared shirt with loud yellow stripes, dark blue shorts, a pair of purple sneakers that looked a size too big for the rest of him.

She felt rather plain in comparison.

"What?" DJ inspected his shoes and shirt, then looked back at her, confused.

Sophia flushed. "Nothing. All right. If you have the Memories, and I have them, and my mom had them the day I was born—maybe it's the *day* that was special. June eleventh. Maybe something happened then. Were you born at the hospital?"

DJ nodded. There was only one hospital in town, so there wasn't any need to clarify.

"We could go," she said, suddenly shy. "To the hospital, I mean. Maybe something special happened that day. I know a nurse there. We could ask. Try to figure something out."

She stared at him, caught between a surge of defiance and a jolt of crippling anxiety, until he nodded.

"Yeah, sure. Why not?"

"Right." Sophia tried to sound like he did. Like it

didn't really matter if they went or not, if he wanted to go with her or not. "Why not."

She blinked rapidly and looked away. Caught Luke watching the two of them. He was much closer than she'd thought—close enough to have heard her conversation.

She narrowed her eyes at him.

He pivoted away, following the rest of their class down the hall.

6

SOPHIA HAD ALREADY BEEN TO THE LOCAL
hospital many times. Once in first grade when she broke
her wrist. Once in third grade when she couldn't stop
throwing up. And then, of course, there was the year her
mother was sick.

"Come on," she called to DJ. He lingered by the
whooshing automatic doors. They'd opened and closed
for him several times already, letting out blasts of frigid
hospital air.

He grimaced but came through the door. "I forgot
the way this place smells."

"Clean?" Sophia said distractedly. She headed for the

front desk, only glancing behind to make sure DJ was keeping up.

"A weird kind of clean." He tugged at the edge of his shirt.

The receptionist gave them a quizzical smile. "Can I help you?"

"Yes, please." Sophia said. "Can I talk with Nurse Loi?"

She knew it helped to be polite in situations like this—to smile as much as possible and look as if you expected no problems getting what you wanted. It was a skill she'd picked up years back, when things had been rougher at home. Her dad hadn't gotten the job at the law office yet, and Sophia had needed to help out more.

"Do you have a family member here at the hospital?" The receptionist cast a glance at DJ, who still looked decidedly leery. "Are your parents around? Or any guardians?"

"Nurse Loi told me to get her if I ever needed any-thing," Sophia said, blustering past the woman's ques-tions. "Can you just tell her that Sophia Wallace is here? She'll come down—I know she will."

The receptionist hesitated. "All right, one minute. I'll give her a call."

She dialed a number and waited while the phone rang. Sophia turned to DJ, who shuffled his feet as his eyes darted around the atrium.

"What's wrong?" she whispered, and he made a face again.

"I hate hospitals," he muttered. "They creep me out."

Sophia looked around, trying to see the creepiness that DJ saw. This hospital wasn't as big or nice as the one in the city, where she'd gone with her mother a time or two. That one had been all shiny steel and flashy windows. Here the walls were faded, and the fish tank in the atrium only had a handful of sleepy, dull-colored fish. But everything was neat and clean where it mattered.

Maybe hospitals should have freaked her out more than they did. If she concentrated, she could still remember the layout of the cancer ward. She could remember waving hello to the nurses and sitting on her mother's hospital bed, staring at the tree of IV fluids pumping into the delicate blue vein of her mother's arm.

But everyone had always been nice to her. And so, despite everything, she'd never found it creepy here at the hospital.

"You didn't have to come," Sophia said.

DJ squared his shoulders. "No, you're right. This is a good place to check out."

Behind them, the receptionist hung up the phone. "Nurse Loi will be down in a moment."

Sophia gave her a bright, bland smile and pulled DJ from the desk before the woman tried to make conversation.

A few minutes later the elevator dinged, and Nurse Loi bustled out, her eyes scanning the atrium for Sophia. The two of them crashed into a hug.

"How are you, my dear?" Nurse Loi wore cheerful pink scrubs, and her short black hair bracketed her face. She was even shorter than Sophia, a tiny woman with a firm grip and a quick, flashing smile. "How's your father? Doing okay?"

Sophia nodded. She stayed pressed against Nurse Loi a moment longer, then grudgingly drew herself away. There was something comforting about the nurse's presence—her peppy scrubs, her steady brown eyes, the way she'd treated Sophia like a friend whenever Sophia had come with her mother.

"This is DJ," Sophia said.

DJ waved. Nurse Loi smiled at him before turning

her attention back to Sophia. "What brings you here today, darling?"

Sophia bit her lip. "Were you working here when I was born?"

Nurse Loi raised an eyebrow and laughed. "How old are you, Sophia? Eleven? Twelve? I've been working here a lot longer than that."

"So you were here that day?"

"Possibly. What're you trying to ask?"

Sophia glanced at DJ. She couldn't very well say, *I think something weird happened here the day I was born. Something that gave my mom and me the ability to see things we shouldn't.*

"Is there anyone who would have been in the room when I was born?" she said awkwardly. "When my mom was pregnant with me, I mean."

Nurse Loi's eyes went soft. Sophia got the uncomfortable itch she felt whenever someone pitied her. She fought the urge to make her escape. She'd come here—had dragged DJ here—for a reason.

"I'm sure we could find someone," Nurse Loi said. "I have a few friends who work in the maternity ward. Shall we go talk to them?"

Once on the maternity ward, Nurse Loi hustled

the two of them toward the nurses' station. A woman screamed from a nearby room. DJ looked vaguely ill, but Nurse Loi barely seemed to notice. She flagged down a woman in bright blue scrubs and asked, "Is Helen around?"

"Right over here," a woman called from down the hall. She gave Nurse Loi a smile as she reached them, then raised her eyebrows at Sophia and DJ. "And who's this?"

"Sophia," Sophia said.

She nudged DJ until he cleared his throat and added, "DJ. DeAndre Johnson."

"Sophia's a special friend of mine," Nurse Loi said. "She spent a lot of time here with her mother a few years ago. She was wondering if any of the nurses here were working the day she was born."

Nurse Loi smiled at Helen in a way that made Sophia realize she expected the answer to be *No*, or *Sorry, we have no idea—that was far too long ago*. That she'd expected an answer like that from the very beginning, and this excursion to the maternity ward was just a placating gesture. A way to humor a little kid with a dead mother because you felt bad for her, and what else could you do?

Sophia's stomach churned. *Never mind,* she was about to say. It was on the tip of her tongue.

Then she realized that Helen wasn't looking at her at all. Or even at Nurse Loi.

She was staring at DJ.

"DeAndre Johnson?" she said, her voice amused. "Has it really been that long?"

DJ's eyebrows rose. It took him a second to find his words. "I'm sorry. Do we—did we meet already?"

Helen laughed. "Oh sure, though I'm not surprised you don't remember. I'm sorry, Sophia, I don't know if I was here the day you were born—but I sure was the day DJ's mama came in."

7

THE STORY OF DJ'S BIRTH WENT LIKE THIS:

Things didn't start out particularly special—*Well, no more special than any child's birth,* Helen amended. DJ's mom was calm, all things considered. She smiled between contractions, chatted with the technicians while they monitored the baby's heartbeat. She talked about the little girl she already had, who was so excited for her baby brother that she couldn't sit still.

The baby himself—DJ—came in the middle of the night. Ten little fingers, ten little toes. Healthy. Perfect. Helen, one of the nurses in the room, was just placing him into his mother's arms when the weirdness started.

"She startled, seeing me," Helen said. "She was

exhausted, of course—but she *jumped* at the sight of me and said, 'Did Devony step out?'"

"Who's Devony?" DJ said. He'd been listening with rapt attention.

"That's what I said," Helen replied. "And your mama, she goes, *The nurse who was here the whole time. Devony.* Now, I'm telling you—there wasn't anybody there except me and Yasmin the whole time. And the doctor. Plus, we don't have anybody named Devony. I don't know if I've ever met someone named Devony. But your mama, she kept insisting that some Nurse Devony had been with her for hours—that they'd talked about everything, that Devony had told her all about the two boys she had at home, and how sometimes the second child came easier . . . anyway, all sorts of things."

DJ was silent, wide-eyed.

"Maybe she was just tired," Nurse Loi said. "A little confused."

Helen shook her head. "Maybe. Except the next morning, after she'd rested and slept, I caught her asking the other nurses if they knew anyone named Devony. She couldn't believe that no one did. It was the strangest thing. Stuck with me, obviously." She looked at DJ. "Your mama never mentioned it to you?"

DJ shook his head, stunned quiet.

Helen turned back to Sophia and Nurse Loi. "I'm sorry—I was on my way to a patient. But I can come back around afterward, if you guys want to stick around for a bit?"

"That's okay," Sophia said, sneaking a look at DJ. "I think we're just going to go."

DJ still looked dazed as Sophia guided him out of the hospital. She had to guide him, because she feared he might run straight into a wall if she didn't. The parking lot was an oven after the chilly hospital atrium. Sophia shuddered in the heat.

"My mother doesn't make things up," DJ said. It was the first thing he'd said, other than a muttered *good-bye* and *thank you* to the nurses, since he'd heard Helen's story. "She doesn't even like fantasy movies and stuff because she thinks they're silly, you know?"

"Sure, sure," Sophia said, dragging him over to the sidewalk. She was already sweating, and they needed to hurry if they were going to catch the next bus home.

"She wouldn't make up something like that. She

wouldn't say something like that unless she was absolutely sure it had happened."

"So it must have happened," Sophia said.

DJ stayed silent, but she could hear the gears turning in his head, grinding in this new information, as she pulled him under the shade of the nearby bus stop.

"Look—" She pressed on his shoulders until he sat obligingly on the metal bench. "It makes sense."

"Does it?"

"Sure," Sophia said patiently. She said it mostly to make DJ feel better, but things *were* starting to fall into place. At least, she thought they were. "We were born on the same day—the day of the eclipse. And there was something special about that day. Something that made my mom see my birth hours before it happened. Something that made your mom talk with a woman who didn't exist. Something, maybe, that gave us our Memories."

"*Something,*" DJ echoed. "But what?"

Sophia didn't have an answer.

A yapping noise interrupted their conversation. A few yards away, a teacup-size terrier dog barked so hard that each *woof* blasted it backward. Its owner, a wiry old woman, looked like she might start snarling soon herself.

The objects of their fury—two teenagers with loud haircuts and razor-sharp smiles—seemed more amused than afraid. The boy adopted a hunched-over, limping walk as they moved away, and his friend laughed mockingly.

Bus Stop Mae, as many of the kids called her, watched them go in stony silence. Mae—no one seemed to know or care about her last name—had been a fixture of this area for as long as Sophia remembered. She might have been sixty or seventy or a hundred. Sophia had never gotten a close look.

Mae never talked to anyone. She never asked for money. Mostly, she just chattered at her raggedy little terrier dog and laughed at jokes only the two of them understood.

"Should we go see if she's okay?" DJ whispered.

Sophia hesitated. Like most of the local kids, she usually avoided looking Mae in the eyes. There was something *off* about her.

Luckily, their bus came before she had to make a decision. They were quiet as they boarded, DJ peering out the window at Mae. He took out his sketchbook as the bus pulled from the curb, flipping through his drawings as if they might help him understand the story he'd heard this afternoon. Sophia left him to his thoughts.

Thirteen years ago, at least two oddities had occurred here, on the day of a partial solar eclipse. In a week, their town was supposed to experience a total eclipse. Did that mean something?

"Eclipses *are* supposed to be harbingers of change." DJ slipped a sheet of notebook paper from his sketchbook. On it were the notes he'd gathered from their last library session. "If it's really all connected somehow, then . . ."

He trailed off, frowning.

"Maybe that's why my Memories are getting more frequent," Sophia said. Her heart thumped. "If they're tied to the solar eclipse—"

A lurch yanked her from her pondering. She launched forward in her seat—threw her hands out to catch herself. Several passengers cried out in alarm.

"You okay?" DJ said, and Sophia nodded as she stood, trying to see what had made the driver stop so suddenly.

He was shouting at someone through the windshield—at a boy who'd darted in front of the bus.

Luke.

8

THE BUS SQUEALED TO A STOP FIVE FEET
from Luke's nose. He stood frozen in the middle of the
road, a black-and-white cat squirming in his arms. His
eyes were wide, his chest heaving.

Sophia squeezed past DJ into the bus's aisle. Yelled at
the red-faced driver that she had to get off right here—
that she knew that boy. That she'd get him off the street.
Grudgingly, the driver opened the door.

Sophia dashed out. DJ followed a step behind.

"Luke?" She slowed as she neared him. The cat in his
arms yowled; she was surprised it hadn't scratched him
yet. "Luke? You have to get out of the street."

He was breathing so hard she heard the rasp of

each inhale, the punch of each exhale. He shook.

"Luke?" Sophia said. "Luke!"

He blinked at her.

His eyes focused.

Without speaking, he turned and walked away in the opposite direction. Sophia ran after him.

He released the cat once he reached a nearby house. It didn't streak off, but looped around Luke's feet in a self-satisfied sort of way.

The bus driver jabbed at his horn.

"Sophia?" DJ said. "I think he's asking if we want to get back on."

Sophia hesitated, watching Luke, who watched his cat. He didn't seem to care if she and DJ stayed or not. In fact, he barely seemed to notice they were there. His breathing had calmed a little, and he no longer trembled, but he didn't seem all right, either.

It felt wrong to leave him alone like this.

The door to the house opened. A man stepped onto the porch. "Luke? You coming back in?" He seemed startled to see Sophia and DJ out on the lawn, but smiled at them. "Who's this?"

Luke acknowledged them with a glance. "We're

working on a project together," he said blandly.

The man waved. "Well, come in, then."

Behind the trio, the bus driver gave up on waiting and drove off.

Sophia looked at DJ, saw her own curiosity reflected on his face. What would Luke McPherson's house be like? What kind of place could contain a boy like that?

Luke didn't meet their eyes, just stared at the stretch of road over their shoulders. "Don't tell him, okay?" he mumbled. "It'll just freak him out. Don't tell him I almost got hit."

He headed for the door without another look back. The cat followed him to the porch but no farther, pacing back and forth on the top step before settling into a sunny spot with its paws outstretched.

The walls of Luke's house were so crowded that it took Sophia a moment to even realize what color they were (pale yellow). Needlepoints of kittens and rainbows rubbed elbows with framed photographs of blond-haired babies, which bumped up against plaques and certificates of all kinds.

MARNI McPHERSON, most of them said.

MARNI McPHERSON, *cheerleader.* MARNI McPHERSON, *pianist.* MARNI McPHERSON, *homecoming princess.*

There were a few certificates for Luke, too, from elementary school. The *Most Likely to* . . . ones awarded to the whole class. In first grade, Luke had apparently been *Most Likely to Join the Circus.* The teasing, colorful certificate didn't seem like something that could ever have been associated with Luke.

His shoulders stayed hunched even inside his own house. If anything, he wound up even tighter, as if the weight of all those plaques and photographs pressed down on him.

"You kids hungry?" Luke's father asked. Sophia assumed it was Luke's father, anyway. His hair was darker than Luke's, brown instead of sandy blond, but they had the same blue eyes and largish nose. He hovered in the foyer while Sophia and DJ took in their surroundings. "Or thirsty? It's blazing out there today, isn't it? We have soda. Or juice—"

"Oh," Sophia said. "Um . . ."

She always got flustered in other people's houses, worried that she might say or do the wrong thing. That

they might decide they'd made a horrible mistake in letting her in, and never invite her back again.

"We're okay, thanks." DJ sounded like he knew what
he was talking about, so Sophia just nodded.

"I'll make you guys some sandwiches, at least," the
man said, and bustled toward the kitchen.

Luke followed him and rummaged around in a cabinet until he produced a can of cat food and a small tin
bowl. He blew past Sophia and DJ without bothering to
look at them, stepping back out to the porch. The door
shut.

"I can text Nicole and ask her to pick us up," DJ whispered.

Instead of answering, Sophia yanked open the front
door and planted herself in the threshold. She stared at
the back of Luke's head.

He crouched by the cat, watching it greedily eat its
way through the bowl of soft food.

"Aren't you going to say anything to us at all?" she
demanded.

She was used to being ignored at school—not dis-
liked, but not particularly liked, either. Just forgotten.
She accepted it. Maybe if she tried harder to talk with

the other kids, to smile and laugh and chat about silly, nothing things with them, they'd like her more.

It was harder to accept Luke's pointed silence, which felt more like an attack than an omission.

He tilted his head up and met her eyes. He looked faintly angry, though Sophia had no idea what he was angry about.

She tensed, preparing herself for anything he might launch at her.

But in the end, all he did was turn back to the cat and run his hand over its head, his fingers scratching gently at the base of its ears.

"We should work on our project," he said.

Luke's bedroom was just as yellow as the rest of the house, and just as crowded. Sophia picked her way past a pile of crumpled clothing, nearly tripped over an abandoned baseball bat, and warned DJ milliseconds before his foot came down on Luke's cell phone.

Luke, seemingly oblivious to the health hazard he lived in, tossed his book bag onto his bed and mumbled about getting snacks before disappearing into the hall again.

Sophia whirled to face DJ as soon as he was gone. "What do you think we should do next?"

"Well," DJ said, "we should decide on a research question, and—"

"About the *Memories*, DJ." Sophia was already bursting with ideas. "We could talk to your mom. Ask to hear her side of the story. What exactly did she see? What else was different about that other version of the hospital?"

"I don't know," DJ said. "What if she asks why we're asking? Or how we even know?"

"We'll just tell her it has to do with the eclipse project," Sophia said. "Like, we're looking into weird events that happened during eclipses or something. We don't have to tell her everything we know."

DJ frowned. "What *do* we know? Right now, all we have to go on is our birthday. And that something strange happened at the hospital."

"And that we see things no one else does." Sophia pulled him down next to her at the foot of Luke's bed. "We have memories of things that never happened, DJ. I have memories of my mom being alive after she died, and you have memories of a stepdad who doesn't even exist. Don't you think we should figure out why? What it means?"

"Of course I do. But Sophia, what if they just are what they are—a weird glitch? Us seeing things we shouldn't. Maybe that's all there is to it."

"What if it *isn't*? If all this started during that eclipse thirteen years ago, maybe it means something that there's going to be another eclipse soon. And maybe—maybe if we don't do everything we can to figure out what's going on, we'll miss our only chance to—"

The rest of her sentence stuck in her throat, too terrifying to release. If she didn't say it out loud, then it wasn't real. And if it wasn't real, then it couldn't disappoint her, couldn't hurt her.

She swallowed. Tried again to spit out the words: "Maybe if we don't do everything we can, we'll miss our only chance to—"

Something crinkled. Sophia's head snapped up.

Luke stood in the doorway, a bag of chips in one hand, a plate of sandwiches in the other. And a look on his face that told Sophia he'd heard everything.

"Our only chance to what?" he demanded.

9

"HAVEN'T YOU EVER HEARD THAT EAVES-
dropping's rude?" Sophia snapped.

Luke's face folded into a frown, the lines of it well-
worn from habitual use. "You're sitting in *my* room. And
anyway, only chance to *what?*"

He turned to DJ when Sophia didn't reply.

"It's nothing," DJ mumbled.

"It's not nothing." Luke glanced into the hall, as if
making sure his father hadn't heard. "You were talking
about the eclipse—"

"For our project," DJ said.

Luke shook his head. "And about memories—seeing
things that weren't real. About—" He jabbed a finger

at Sophia. "About her mom still being alive, and you having a stepdad. You were talking about it at school too. I heard you."

He glared at them, daring them to disagree. He was as tense as he had been out on the road, staring down a ten-ton bus.

Instinct goaded Sophia onto the offensive. "I don't know what you're going on about."

Luke gave her a withering look.

DJ cleared his throat. "Since we're all here, we should figure out how we're going to split up our project—"

"I know someone," Luke said. "An astrophysicist. I bet whatever it is you're trying to figure out, he could help. He's been researching eclipses and—and some kind of weirdness—as long as I've known him. I've seen his library. He's got tons of books and notes and everything."

DJ and Sophia exchanged a look. They couldn't help it.

"What do you mean, you know this guy?" DJ said slowly.

"He lives a couple streets down," Luke said. "That was his cat I saved from the bus."

Sophia wasn't ready to forgive Luke for intruding on their conversation.

"Why do you care?" she said.

Luke didn't seem offended. But he didn't answer, either. At least, not verbally. His eyes went to the hallway outside his room.

To the crowded yellow walls.

To all the plaques and certificates that still hung on the walls after three years, remembrances of a girl forever seventeen.

"I don't know what's going on. But if you're seeing your dead mom, and DJ's seeing his stepdad . . ." He took a deep breath. "I want my life back. I want things to be the way they were before."

Luke's father stopped smiling the minute he heard that Luke wanted to leave the house. Sophia and DJ maintained a polite distance while the two of them argued. Finally they must have reached a compromise, because Luke scooped the cat into his arms and stalked away.

"Don't be gone too long," his father shouted after him. "Your mother will be home soon!"

Luke ignored him. Sophia and DJ mumbled awkward good-byes, then made their escape as well.

"Your dad seems nice," DJ offered, once they'd caught up with Luke.

Luke grunted. Sophia didn't say anything, because while his dad had seemed nice, he'd also seemed a little overbearing. Her own dad had never fussed about where Sophia went, or why, or when. She knew it worried him if she was out too late, or if she didn't check in, so she never strayed too far.

But she never felt babied, either. Her dad trusted her. Relied on her when he wasn't able to rely on anyone else. She'd always been proud of that.

"Does it have a name?" she asked, once they'd walked in silence for a while. "The cat."

"Schrödinger," Luke said. He didn't offer up anything more.

The houses along Luke's street were squat and neat, with pretty lawns and brightly colored curtains. As they walked farther down the block and turned onto a side road, the gaps between the houses grew wider. The lawns grew scraggly, and less profusely green.

"How do you know this guy?" DJ said, studying their surroundings.

Luke forged onward. Sophia had never seen him

this focused before. "The first time Schrödinger came to my house, we found some 'Missing' posters around, with Mr. Scot's phone number on them. My mom called, and he came to get the cat. But Schrödinger kept getting loose, and after a while, I started just taking him home."

As he spoke, he turned into the driveway of a particularly run-down-looking blue house. He plopped Schrödinger on the front stoop, then jabbed the doorbell.

The man who stuck his head out looked far better groomed than his home. His curly hair was artfully styled, his button-down crisp against his warm brown skin. He looked younger than Sophia expected an astrophysicist to look.

"There you are," he said to Schrödinger. The cat strolled indoors, its tail flicked high.

Luke didn't seem bothered by the lack of hello. "I fed him," he said.

Both of them watched the cat. Mr. Scot made a *hmm* sort of sound, contemplative. Then his gaze moved to Sophia and DJ. His eyebrows rose, but he didn't ask questions, just waited.

"That's Sophia and DJ." Luke sounded far less

impatient than he had when he'd semi-introduced them to his father.

"Hello, Sophia," Mr. Scot said slowly. "Hello, DJ."

He stayed in the doorway, not inviting them in, but not shutting the door, either. Still waiting, obviously, for more information. Sophia felt an answer pressing inside her, but she waited for Luke to speak. He was the one who knew this man. Who'd know what to say.

"We want to know about solar eclipses," said Luke.

Even once he'd let them inside, Mr. Scot seemed wary, as if he'd just invited wild animals into his home, and at any moment, they might bite or make a mess.

"Is this for a school project?" he said.

"Yes," Sophia said quickly. She had no reason to trust this man yet. The less he knew, the better.

Mr. Scot led them to a small, cluttered kitchen. It was overstuffed with things that normally didn't belong in kitchens—hardcover books with missing dust jackets, grimy old CD cases, even what looked like a typewriter.

"Then you should be at a library." He filled a rusty kettle with water. "Isn't that where kids go for school projects?"

"But you're a direct source," Luke said. "You know everything about eclipses."

Mr. Scot's fingers twitched nervously around his horn-rimmed glasses. "What do you mean, everything?"

"Well, you've got all that research," Luke said. "And you have so many books on it—like that one." He pointed behind Mr. Scot, who jerked around. The kettle in his hand tilted, splashing water onto the kitchen floor—and onto Schrödinger. The cat yowled, twisting midair before hightailing it out of the kitchen.

Mr. Scot cursed. "Is the front door closed? Close the door—quickly!"

DJ rushed to do just that while Sophia darted after the terrified cat. Before she knew it, she'd careened into a stuffy old library. Schrödinger slipped underneath an armchair, melting into the darkness.

The library was even messier than the kitchen. Mr. Scot had nailed a corkboard to one wall, then covered it with a mess of newspaper clippings and handwritten notes. Books littered not only the bookshelves, but the end tables, and even the floors. Some were brand-new, their dust covers crisp. Others had foxed edges and yellowing pages.

Sophia couldn't help but read the titles: *Sun Shadow, Eclipses of the Twentieth Century, Passage, Eclipse: Myths and Beyond*. No wonder Luke thought Mr. Scot knew everything there was to know about eclipses.

A tattered notebook sat facedown on the armchair. Someone—Mr. Scot?—had jotted a title on the cover. Sophia squinted at the loopy script. *The Universes, This One and Beyond*. Was Mr. Scot writing a book?

She moved closer, was just about to pick up the notebook, when her eyes caught on a picture hanging on the wall. It wasn't large, barely bigger than Sophia's hand. In it, a young woman bent over a fat-bodied cello, pulling music from its strings.

She was lovely, all dark curls and slender fingers. The camera had caught just a portion of her face, but even so, Sophia could tell this woman *felt* the notes she played.

She paused without realizing she'd stopped. Stood there looking at the portrait, and almost heard the music.

"There you are," Mr. Scot said from the doorway. He didn't look pleased. DJ and Luke crowded on either side of him, DJ's eyes sweeping hungrily around the library. *See?* Luke's face said. *Didn't I tell you?*

Sophia pointed at the portrait. "Who's that?" she

asked, trying to buy DJ more time. Maybe he'd see something she hadn't. "Do you know her?"

Maybe it was just an impersonal portrait, something he'd bought because it was pretty. But Sophia watched as Mr. Scot's eyes shifted to the picture, and she didn't think that was the case.

"That's a complicated question," he said. "Come on, time for you guys to go home."

He ushered the boys from the library door and stared at Sophia until she grudgingly came toward him. But not before casting one last glance at the corkboard. Most of the print was too small to read from a distance, but she managed to snag a single headline—THE MYSTERY OF DONWAY SHALLOWS.

That was all she got before Mr. Scot nudged her out of the way and shut the library doors.

10

LUKE SHADOWED SOPHIA AND DJ ALL THE
way back to his house. He was supposed to be leading
the way, since it was his house and all, but he kept looping around so he could stare at them, could say, "What
do you think? I told you he was an astrophysicist."

Sophia had no idea how to handle his sudden, force-
ful attention. She sort of wished he'd just go back to
being sullen. At least he was easier to ignore that way.

"He didn't tell us anything," she said.

"Yeah, but you saw his library! And Mr. Scot's just
like that at first. He'll warm up to you. Kind of."

"Did you see that stuff on the corkboard?" Sophia
asked DJ. "The newspaper clippings and notes?"

He nodded. "It was weird. There was something about how one place was super cold even though it was noon, and it had rained, but everything was dry. I don't know. Maybe it's his research."

"Did you see anything about your memories?" Luke asked. "Any references or hints?"

Sophia didn't like the way he slipped *Memories* so haphazardly into the conversation, as if he knew what he was talking about. It must have shown on her face, because Luke pressed his mouth shut.

"I did introduce you to him." He was starting to look grumpy again. He didn't say, *What about your end of the deal?* In fact, Sophia hadn't agreed to any sort of deal at all. But she was a fair-minded sort of girl, and she understood the way of unspoken bargains.

"When were you born?" she said slowly.

He squinted at her. "Why?"

"Was it June eleventh?" DJ said, cutting to the point.

Luke shook his head.

"So you wouldn't have the Memories," Sophia said.

In a way, she was relieved. She liked that the Memories were something only she and DJ shared, something special between the two of them. She wasn't sure if she was ready to share that with anyone else. Especially someone as ornery as Luke.

"I have *memories*," he said. "I have lots of memories—"

Sophia tried to interrupt, to tell him that that wasn't what she was getting at, but he bulldozed over her.

"I have nine *years* of memories," he snapped.

That shut Sophia right up. Whether or not he'd meant to, he'd hurt her. Hit her in the soft, underbelly parts where her armor didn't reach.

Sophia might have Memories—strange, magical, surreal—but Luke had just plain *memories*.

Solid. Real.

He didn't have to question what they meant. Didn't have to wonder at their source. He'd spent nine whole *real* years with his sister, and that was something no amount of Memories could replace.

"Good for you," Sophia said coldly.

Luke shut his mouth, but he didn't apologize. They glared at each other, two unmovable forces unwilling to yield.

They might have stood there the rest of the evening, their mutual stubbornness riding out the sunset and the moonrise. But things didn't get that far. If only because, just then, a gleaming red convertible pulled up beside them.

"Time to go, kids," Nicole drawled. She'd flung one arm across the driver's-side window, and the other was draped lazily across the steering wheel. Her aviator sunglasses shone honey gold in the afternoon sun, her Afro tucked behind a fuchsia scarf.

"Come on, Sophia," DJ said, and tugged her arm when she didn't move.

Sophia stood her ground for a moment longer, loath to yield before Luke. But Nicole was waiting, and Luke might as well have been a statue. Sophia tilted her chin up and stalked toward the car.

She'd never been this close to Nicole or her car before. The convertible was even shinier than she'd thought, as if it were lovingly buffed and waxed every day. Nicole herself was just as glamorous, with a silver bangle on each brown wrist, and brick-red lipstick. Either she or the car seats smelled faintly of vanilla.

Nicole didn't raise her shades as her brother and Sophia climbed into the car. She didn't acknowledge Luke at all, just left him in her dust as she screeched off.

"Sophia lives on Pine Oak." DJ had to yell to be heard

over the wind roaring by. Nicole nodded once to show she'd heard.

In the backseat, Sophia was still cooling down from her standoff with Luke. DJ twisted around to face her—and probably to check if she was okay.

"So, what did you see on Mr. Scot's board?" he said.

If he was trying to distract her, it worked. Sophia's mind zoomed back to Mr. Scot's library.

"'The Mystery of Donway Shallows,'" she recited.

"Donway Shallows?" Nicole said. "What about Donway Shallows?"

"What do *you* know about it?" asked Sophia.

Nicole pushed her sunglasses up so they sat atop her curls like a crown. Her eyes were big and deep brown like DJ's; they glinted as she raised her eyebrows at Sophia in the rearview mirror. "It's that old textile mill at the edge of town. Out in the woods? It's a bit of a party place during the summer. Why? You two have no business being out there."

"No reason," DJ said.

Nicole gave him a skeptical look and blew through a yellow light just before it turned red. Soon they reached Sophia's street.

"Which house is yours?" Nicole asked.

"It's just a little farther down," Sophia said, and directed Nicole to her driveway.

Her father's car sagged by the tiny, square lawn. It had never been fancy, but it looked shabbier than ever next to the well-loved, shiny red of Nicole's convertible. Sophia tried not to look at it too much, as if by keeping it out of her gaze, she could keep it out of DJ's and Nicole's as well.

"Want to go check it out this weekend?" DJ whispered as she passed by the front seat. "The mill?"

She'd just been trying to work up the nerve to ask him the same thing, and grinned as she nodded.

"Bye," he called out.

They screeched off in a cloud of exhaust, leaving Sophia alone outside her house.

11

IT WAS QUIET WHEN SHE OPENED THE
door, no TV playing, no sounds of her dad putting
together an early dinner so they could eat before he left
for work. It was a lot later than Sophia had expected to
get home. Her dad was probably worried by now.

She didn't shout for him, because the silence meant
he could be napping. Her dad was always sneaking sleep
into the nooks and crannies of the day. Sometimes,
Sophia caught him nodding off in the middle of TV
shows.

She padded through the hall and peeked into the living room. He'd fallen asleep on the couch, the TV flashing silently in the background.

An envelope lay on the coffee table, next to a half-eaten bowl of cereal. Sophia eased the bowl away from the edge of the table so it wouldn't topple. She didn't mean to peek at the envelope—she assumed it was a bill statement, or something from work.

But her eyes caught on it nonetheless. It was old, one corner stained, the edges worn from touch.

Curiosity pushed her closer. She glanced at her father's face, making sure he was asleep. He was out cold. A frown tugged at his eyebrows. When her father was awake, he'd smile at her, even when he was tired. When he was asleep, he somehow seemed even more exhausted.

The envelope contained only a single sheet of paper. A letter, written in messy cursive.

It took Sophia a moment to recognize her mother's handwriting.

She wouldn't have recognized it at all, if it weren't for the stolen Memories.

I shouldn't, she thought, even as she smoothed out the folds in the letter. This could be private. *Was* private.

But bigger than the guilt was a sudden anger that her father had kept this from her. Sophia had no letters from her mother. She had a few stuffed animals, and a plastic bracelet from the hospital gift shop, and memories.

Rob, the letter began. No *Dear,* no *Hello,* just her father's name stark in black pen.

Rob—

She didn't get any further than that.

Her father woke. Woke and tore the letter from her hand, so sudden and harsh that Sophia jerked backward— was certain the paper had cut her, and that she might be bleeding.

It hadn't. She wasn't. But she looked at her father, at his wide-open eyes, and hurt nonetheless.

"Sophia—" he said, his voice gravelly from sleep.

But she couldn't talk to him right then. She couldn't speak. She thought, suddenly, that she might cry.

She fled to her room. The door shut with satisfying finality—shut her in and the rest of the world out.

"Sophia?" Her father's voice came muffled through the door.

Sophia curled into herself on the floor beside her bed—the side opposite the door, where she couldn't see it and could pretend it didn't exist.

Of course, she couldn't do that very well when her dad kept knocking.

"Sophia, can I come in?"

He sounded sorry instead of mad. Sophia had been afraid he might be mad about the letter. But she was mad too. How dare he yank the letter away when those were *her* mother's words. She had a right to them as much as he did.

But they weren't for you, the traitorous, reasonable part of her said. She shoved it aside, too angry and sad and aching to listen. It all washed over her, a tantrum of things she didn't want to feel but did.

In a couple of weeks, Sophia would turn thirteen. And once she did, she'd have lived more years without her mother than she had with her.

Every year after that would skew the scales even more. She couldn't stop that. But it would be nice to have something to hold on to.

"I'm coming in, Sophia," her father said.

The door creaked open. Her dad folded himself down next to her on the carpet. He was still wearing his red Tom's Diner shirt, and smelled faintly like french fries and maple syrup.

Sophia curled up tighter and tighter and tighter until she couldn't hold it anymore, until her muscles ached and she had to release them, unwind them one by one as her breathing slowed and her heart quieted. Still, they sat and didn't look at each other.

She wished he would say something. Would speak first. Would ask her if she was okay, or why she was upset, or if she wanted to talk about things.

She wasn't sure what she'd say in reply. Wasn't sure she could even put everything into words.

But it would be nice if he asked.

He never asked. He boxed up unhappy things the way he'd boxed up all traces of Sophia's mother.

"You were late coming back from school today," he said.

Sophia shrugged. She had her knees pressed against her chest, her arms wrapped around herself.

"Hanging out with friends?" He was always saying stuff like that, like he thought Sophia had a bunch of secret friends she wasn't telling him about.

Only today, it had actually been sort of true. She and DJ were friends, anyway. She wasn't quite sure what Luke counted as.

She nodded. It was easier than speaking. Especially when the only thing she wanted to say was, *Can we talk about Mom again? Like we did yesterday?*

Can you tell me something else about her?

What was in the letter?

Are there more letters?

Are there any for me?

But the words stuck in her throat, and she was still trying to swallow around them when her dad squeezed her shoulder, and hesitated, and stood.

"How's spaghetti for dinner sound?" he said. "Come out here and help me?"

She nodded again. Her dad only had a couple more hours before work. She shouldn't ruin it by being upset.

But sometimes, it was hard to help it.

He left, and she stayed there, staring at the floor.

12

BY THE END OF MR. RAE'S CLASS ON FRIDAY,
Sophia, DJ, and Luke had settled on a title for their
project: "Solar Eclipses and the Destruction of the
Established Order" (DJ had come up with it), decided
on their sources, and were mostly done divvying up the
workload.

DJ and Sophia had also mapped out their excursion
to Donway Shallows. The plan was to tell Sophia's dad
that she'd gone to DJ's to work on their project. DJ's mom
had a book club meeting every Sunday morning, so the
only person at home would be Nicole. And Nicole, DJ
assured Sophia, could be bribed to keep quiet.

He told her this last bit with a conspiring grin.

Last week, Sophia would have never in a million years expected to see such a look on DJ's face. DJ Johnson, who'd always seemed so serious and above it all. Now he was her partner in crime.

And Luke—well. Luke was being helpful with the project. He looked things up on the websites DJ suggested and wrote down pertinent books from their library. He didn't bring up the bad blood he and Sophia had stirred up after their visit to Mr. Scot.

In fact, he acted like that whole afternoon with Mr. Scot had never happened.

It was impossible, as always, to figure out what he was thinking. But at least he wasn't causing any trouble.

"Should we invite Luke?" Sophia whispered to DJ as they packed up during afternoon announcements.

He looked at her in surprise. "To Donway?"

It seemed stupid now that she'd said it aloud. She'd been looking forward to going alone with DJ. To not having sullen, angry, snappish Luke come along. But it didn't seem fair to leave him behind. After all, if it weren't for Luke, they never would have gone to see Mr. Scot. They never would have known to go to Donway Shallows to begin with.

"I guess we should," she said grudgingly. "Right?"

DJ made a face but nodded.

Luke, as usual, sat slumped in a corner by himself. The other kids in their class chatted heedlessly over the afternoon announcements. He fiddled with a broken pencil.

Sophia gritted her teeth as they approached. Extending this invitation felt like losing. Like being the first to wave a white flag. Still, fair was fair. She swallowed her pride.

"DJ and I are going to go to Donway Shallows on Sunday," she said. Luke looked up but didn't stop fidgeting with his pencil. "You can come if you want."

He scrunched up his nose. "Why're you going there?"

"Mr. Scot had something about it on his wall," DJ said. "A newspaper clipping."

"The point is, there might be a clue," Sophia said. "Do you want to come or not?"

"I don't have the Memories," Luke said quietly. "I wasn't born during an eclipse."

He sounded so upset that Sophia felt a pang of guilt. She hadn't meant to make him feel this bad. She knew what it was like to miss someone. To hate the world for taking them away.

"Maybe it won't matter," she said, as gently as she could. "You won't know unless you try."

"My parents—"

Sophia sighed. "Do you want to come or not, Luke?"

"Fine," he huffed. "I'm coming."

The old textile mill wasn't far from Jessup Middle. Sophia met DJ and Luke in the back parking lot Sunday morning, and they made the rest of the trek together. DJ brought his sketchbook. Luke brought a particularly skeptical frown.

They talked a little as they walked, but mostly they were quiet. A comfortable, companionable quiet. Luke's frown eased into something like curiosity as they roamed farther from the center of town.

Sophia glanced at DJ from time to time and caught him looking at her, too. Each time, both of them broke into surprised, reflexive smiles.

Donway Shallows sat in one of the many historic corners around their little town. *Historic* was the tourist-friendly term for them, anyway. Sophia's dad always laughed when someone called Donway Shallows *historic*.

It's run-down, that's what it is, he'd say. *Calling it historic is like calling a patch of weeds a garden.*

But Sophia didn't think *historic* was the wrong word. The area around Donway Shallows had been full of shops and homes once upon a time, when the textile mill had been open. Walking through it, she saw scraps of bright pink paint spelling out MIMI'S BEAUTY SALON, and the boarded-up windows of a dance hall.

No one lived here anymore except the odd man or woman sleeping on doorsteps, but it must have been quite the place once upon a time. Full of people and noise and color.

Now history was all that remained.

It was midmorning by the time they reached the mill itself. It sat in a dip of land, nestled by a creek that used to power its long-rusted engines. Sunlight streamed through the trees and glinted off the mill's cracked and shattered windowpanes, the skeletal remains of its walls.

A NO TRESPASSING sign stood crookedly a dozen yards from the building, so heavily graffitied that it all blended together. None of them paid it any mind, though DJ did say, "Careful," as they moved beneath the shadow of the mill's tenuous roof. "There's glass everywhere."

Despite the sign, the building showed definite signs of human visitation. Cigarette butts littered patches of sunlight like strange plant life, and Sophia almost tripped over a half-buried beer bottle.

"It's cold." Sophia rubbed at her arms. It had been hot the whole way here, sweat sticking her hair to her neck, and now, somehow, it was cold.

"It's all the trees," DJ said, craning his head back. But Sophia wasn't so sure.

Luke rested his hand on one of the naked, rust-orange struts, rubbing the grit of it beneath his palm.

The woods and the mill were so silent that when Sophia first heard the crunch of underbrush, it shattered the air like gunshots. She froze. A gang of teenagers stomped into the clearing: three boys and two girls. All paused in their raucous laughter when they caught sight of Sophia and DJ and Luke.

They were high schoolers, probably Nicole's age or a little older. One of them jerked his chin at DJ and said, to nobody in particular, "Hey, isn't that Nicole Johnson's little brother?"

It didn't seem a particularly friendly sort of question, and Sophia felt the shift in DJ immediately, the way he went cold and quiet and still. He was the solemn stranger in the corner of the classroom again, too aloof for words.

"You an artist?" the same boy said, coming closer. There was nothing overtly threatening about him. Nothing Sophia could put into words, or explain to an adult. Just a cutting edge to his smile, an arrogant jaunt to his walk. The feeling that he could punch you in the stomach and laugh and say it was just a joke, come on, lighten up, why are you such a *child*?

DJ's shoulders came up, his grip tightening around his sketchbook. He shrugged.

Sophia wanted to say, *Come on, let's go*, but she wasn't sure if that would make things worse.

"What're you doing here?" one of the girls asked. She was beautiful, tall and red-haired, with the air of an exotic bird. She stared Sophia too hard in the eyes, and smiled at her like Sophia was six.

"Hooking up," her friend mock whispered, and the two of them dissolved into crowlike laughter again. One of the guys said, "*Jesus*, Dani, they're like *babies*."

The first boy took advantage of DJ's flush of embarrassment to grab his sketchbook. DJ jerked back. The sketchbook ripped between them, splitting halfway down the spine with a horrible, torn-cloth sound.

Sheets of sketches fluttered to the ground.

The older boy immediately stepped back, holding up his hands. He grinned. "Whoa, sorry, kid. I just wanted a look."

The redheaded girl snatched up a sheet of drawings. Sophia caught a flash of the doodles and felt her heart squeeze. They were sketches of DJ's stepfather.

"Who's this?" the girl said. "Your daddy?"

"Dani," said the same boy who'd chastised her before. "Don't be insensitive."

"What—" Dani whined. Then her eyes brightened. "*Ohhh*. Right."

DJ opened his mouth but made no sound. In that moment, he seemed incapable of words.

It was Luke who snarled, "Give that back," and ripped the drawings from Dani's hands. He was nearly as tall as she was, with his new, growth-spurt height, and she jumped back warily.

She knew who he was. Sophia could tell from the look on her face. As long as Luke lived in this town, he would always be dead Marni McPherson's little brother.

Just like Sophia and DJ, he was defined by something entirely out of his control.

Sophia straightened her shoulders and refused to

look away when one of the older boys stared her down.

DJ was still silent. Luke radiated his usual Luke-ness in all its prickly, angry glory. Sophia had never appreciated it as much as she did now. It wasn't just pointless rage after all—it was a shield.

"Come on," Dani said finally. "This is boring. Let's get out of here."

She flounced off, and her friends followed. By the time they'd disappeared from sight, they'd moved on to a new source of entertainment. Their laughter reverberated through the trees. Then that, too, melted away, and Donway Shallows was quiet again.

DJ kicked at a pile of rocks. His sketchbook was under his arm, the crack down the spine a stark white line in the black cover. Sophia wanted to ask if he was okay but didn't know how.

Maybe he didn't want to talk about it. Maybe he didn't like to think about his dad at all, or what he'd done, or the fallout that had followed.

"Here," Luke said. He held out DJ's sheet of drawings. It was slightly the worse for wear, the length of it crumpled and smudged with dirt.

"Thanks," DJ said dully. He pressed the drawings

back into his sketchbook, careful to lay the page flat before closing the cover.

"Forget about them," Sophia said, with more vitriol than she'd meant to. She cleared her throat, embarrassed.

"Yeah," DJ muttered.

"So what're we actually looking for here?" Luke flung his arms out, gesturing at Donway Shallows at large.

Sophia was still preoccupied with this new, withdrawn version of DJ. She shrugged. "Look for anything out of place, I guess."

Luke took her words to heart. He bustled around them, a whirlwind of energy. One minute, he was at the far end of the mill, clambering onto a pile of rubble. The next, he was out under the trees again, thrashing a stick against the underbrush.

"I might not go to Holden," DJ said, as they watched him.

Holden was the local high school that Jessup Middle fed into. All the kids Sophia knew were going to end up at Holden, mixed in with kids from one of the farther-away middle schools.

Even a lot of the adults Sophia knew had gone to Holden, once upon a time. Her mom and dad had started dating their sophomore year there and married soon after graduation. They'd had Sophia not long after that.

"There's this magnet school I'm going to apply to next year," DJ said. He didn't look at her.

"That's cool," Sophia said, and meant it. High school was a year off in the future. Sometimes that felt frighteningly soon, but most of the time, it was still eons away. There was still the rest of seventh grade, and the summer, and all of eighth grade to get through first.

DJ shrugged. "It's kind of far. All the way out in Rendell. Nicole says it's a whole different crowd out there."

When Sophia thought of Rendell, she thought of the lawyers who worked in the building her father cleaned. Nicole's red convertible wouldn't seem out of place there.

She thought about the older kids who'd just vacated the mill, and the way they'd looked at DJ, and the way DJ had looked at them, and said, "A different crowd might not be a bad thing, I guess."

"I guess," DJ echoed. He cradled his sketchbook in his arms. "They wouldn't know me at all. Or—well, you know."

Or your dad, Sophia thought. She nodded.

DJ looked away. "It's not even that bad for me. It was a

lot worse for Nicole. I mean, it was her teacher he ran off with. But Nicole doesn't let stuff get to her. Nicole laughs at them, and says the only reason they're so hung up on it is because their brains are too small to think about important things."

Sophia laughed, and he smiled, just a little.

"It's probably true," she said.

"Probably," he agreed. "Still . . ."

Still, it didn't make it any easier to endure.

"I know," said Sophia.

Luke was investigating a pile of sheet metal now, which mostly consisted of him trying to pull the pile apart. The pieces of metal must have been heavier than they looked, because he wasn't making much progress. He wedged his fingers underneath a particularly big piece and grunted as he heaved.

"Could you not?" said a voice calmly.

Luke yelped and tipped backward, his arms windmilling for balance.

And out from beneath the sheet metal, cool as could be, emerged Bus Stop Mae.

13

LUKE ROCKETED BACK TO HIS FEET, HIS eyes glued to Mae as she straightened. Despite the warm weather, the old woman wore long sleeves and long pants. Her straggly white curls flopped about her head.

"Those kids gone yet?" Her voice was thick and gravelly, as if seasoned by smoke. Her eyes were dark, vivid blue.

Sophia came to stand beside Luke. DJ flanked him on the other side. Neither boy spoke.

Sophia had never talked to Mae before. It was even more intimidating than she'd expected. She swallowed. "Which kids? The ones who were just here?"

Mae nodded. "They freak out Jimmy. Don't they, Jimmy?"

Jimmy, apparently, was Mae's terrier. He'd been silent all this time, but he yipped up a storm now. Sophia tried not to flinch. The terrier was tiny, and his tail was wagging, but she'd been dog-shy ever since her neighbor's dog had nearly bitten her last year.

Mae smiled. Sophia hadn't known the lady smiled at anyone but her dog. "He likes you," she told Sophia. "No need to be scared."

"I'm not," Sophia said.

Mae tickled her dog underneath the jaw. Her hands were papery white, blotched with liver spots. "What're you kids doing here? Aren't you a bit young for the kind of partying that goes on around these parts?"

"What're *you* doing here?" Sophia countered.

"I live here, thank you very much," Mae said.

"*Here?*" Luke said. "Underneath the metal?"

"It's one of many homes." Mae sounded a bit haughty about it. "Why, you jealous?"

Luke didn't seem to know what to say to that. He shut up.

"It's a nice home," DJ said quietly, and was rewarded

with a guileless smile. "Seems peaceful. I mean, when there aren't people walking all about."

Mae laughed. "I don't know about *peaceful*. But it's certainly got a special kind of energy to it."

"What do you mean?" DJ asked.

Mae folded herself onto the ground and beckoned for the three of them to follow suit. Sophia tensed as Jimmy snuffled over to her knee. Mae gesticulated at nothing in particular—the crumbling mill, the whispering trees, the cigarette-littered dirt. She raised an eyebrow as if to say, *See?*

"I don't feel any kind of energy," Luke said.

"*Shhh*," Mae hissed. "Give it a moment."

Sophia felt about as skeptical as Luke looked. But she was already here on the ground, so it didn't hurt to give it a try. She sat very still and let her eyes wander around the clearing, focusing on nothing in particular. Listening to nothing in particular.

Her breathing deepened. Her shoulders unknotted.

She shivered, struck by a sudden chill. It shouldn't have been this cold, but it was.

And it only got colder. She trembled. Tried to speak, but her tongue wouldn't unstick from the roof of her mouth. Tried to swallow, but couldn't.

"Sophia?" DJ said.

And then he was gone.

He, Luke, Mae—all of Donway Shallows melted away.

Sophie? said Sophia's mother. *Sophie, darling, they're going to start without you.*

The rest of the Memory roared into being. She was at school. She was in the auditorium. The overhead lights flashed twice—a signal. Something was about to start.

A show. No, a performance.

A choir performance.

"I'm in choir," she said, then smacked her hand over her mouth because she'd *spoken*. This was a Memory and she'd actually *spoken*. Sure, sometimes she said things in Memories, but it was like reciting lines from a play. Like watching yourself say something. These words had been real and spontaneous.

Her mother laughed. She was dolled up in a crisp yellow dress and red lipstick. The other parents around them were all dressed up too. *What're you going on about? Go—they're waiting for you backstage.*

Sophia had loved choir when she was a little girl. Her parents had gone to every recital, no matter how small.

Then her mom had gotten sick. Sophia had sung for a year or two after that, but it hadn't felt the same.

Every recital, she'd look for her mother in the audience.

And every recital, her throat would close up.

It wasn't much use being in choir if you couldn't ever sing.

Sophie! her mom whispered. The lights were dimming.

"I'm going, I'm going," Sophia whispered back. She reached out, and her mother met her halfway, squeezing her into a hug.

You're going to do great, darling, she said. *Now go!*

Sophia flashed her a grin, then turned and ran down the darkened aisle. Her skirt fluttered against her legs. The other parents smiled at her as she passed.

I have a solo, she thought as she approached the stage. She hadn't remembered until now. That was why she'd gone to see her mom before the show. She'd been nervous because she had a solo—a big one.

She was going to sing—

She was going to sing—

"Sophia," DJ said. He shook her again, then jumped back as she slapped his hands away, breathing hard, the brightness of Donway Shallows too piercing, too much. She wrapped her arms around herself, gulping for air.

"You guys need to call an ambulance," Mae said. Her eyebrows were drawn, her mouth pursed. "She's having some sort of seizure—"

DJ shook his head, distraught. "It's not a seizure. It's hard to explain. She's fine. Sophia, you're fine, aren't you?"

Sophia couldn't reply. She wasn't fine.

It had been *so real*. The Memories had been getting longer, clearer, for months. But even then, they'd always borne the smudged edges and echoing sound of something one step removed from reality. A lucid dream.

This had been nothing like that.

This had been real. Had felt real.

Only now, as Sophia took heaving breaths and shuddered, her eyes darting around the clearing, she knew it hadn't been.

She was still right where she'd started.

In the real world, whether she wanted to be there or not.

14

"YOU TWO NEED TO CALL AN AMBULANCE,"
Mae kept saying. "Your friend needs to get to a hospital,
get checked out by a doctor."

DJ alternated between throwing Sophia worried
looks and trying to appease Mae. "She's fine. She does
this sometimes. Don't worry."

Mae didn't look convinced. "You all right, girl?" she
asked Sophia.

Sophia's ears rang with the opening notes of the solo
she was supposed to sing. The song she couldn't remember beyond those first few bars.

She closed her eyes, trying to claw her way back into
that world. Back into the darkened school auditorium.

The hushed waiting before the show. The delicious fluttering in her stomach, knowing that in a few minutes, all
eyes would be on her.

The comfort of knowing that her mother was in the
audience, wearing her fancy yellow dress and the world's
biggest grin.

"*Sophia,*" Luke said.

Her eyes snapped open.

"You have a history of seizures?" Mae said.

"No." Sophia climbed to her feet. She had to get out
of here—get away from Mae's questioning. She needed
space to think. "I just space out sometimes. It's nothing."

"Come on," she said under her breath to DJ, "let's go."

He hesitated but nodded, pulling Luke to his feet.
"We'll get out of your way," he told Mae. "Thanks for
having us over."

"You get that girl checked out!" Mae yelled as they
hurried away.

Luke rounded on them as soon as they were out of Mae's
earshot. "What was that?" he demanded.

Sophia tried to ignore him, pushing her way through
the woods, but he wouldn't have it.

"Was it a Memory? Was that it?"

"Yeah, it was," DJ said. "Sophia—slow down. What happened? What did you see?"

"Choir," Sophia whispered.

"What?" DJ said.

"Was it because we were at the mill?" Luke said. "Is that why you had a Memory?"

There were too many voices, too many people.

You're going to do great, darling, said Sophia's mother.

Sophia burst back onto the main road. Skidded to a stop as a truck rattled by, almost hitting her. The driver cursed, hollering for her to watch where she was going.

By the time DJ and Luke caught up, she was calm again. At least on the outside.

"I'm going to go home," she told them.

"All right," DJ said placatingly. Any other time, she might have been annoyed—she didn't like to be placated— but right now, she was just relieved no one argued.

They headed back toward the center of town, Sophia leading the way. Behind her, the boys spoke quietly to each other. She couldn't hear everything, but she caught enough to know they were talking about the Memories. DJ seemed be filling Luke in on the details.

They reached the turn for Luke's house first.

"Thanks," he said suddenly, out of the blue. Not to DJ, but to Sophia.

Sophia frowned. "For what?"

"I don't know." He shrugged and scratched at his hand, embarrassed. "For inviting me today."

He rushed off before Sophia could reply.

DJ and Sophia continued onward. It was full noon now, the sun sweltering. DJ didn't speak, just strolled along beside Sophia, solid and steady and comforting. He didn't ask any questions, didn't pressure her to talk before she was ready.

Little by little, her breathing slowed. She stopped clenching her fists.

"I was at the auditorium," she said quietly.

DJ looked up. "At school?"

"Yeah. In the Memory. There was a performance going on—or about to start. My mom was there."

"Were you going to sing?"

She smiled a little. "I had a solo."

"No way," he said. "That's awesome."

Maybe he was just being nice, but she grinned at him anyway.

"It was so clear, DJ. It was just like real life. It's never been that clear before."

"You were out of it for a really long time," DJ said. "Usually I just blank out for a couple seconds, but you were staring at nothing for, like, half a minute. Maybe more."

Sophia scuffed her shoes against the ground. "I wish it lasted longer."

DJ nodded. They walked a little farther.

"You want to come have lunch?" he asked.

Sophia looked at him in surprise. "What, at your house?"

He shrugged. "Yeah. If you want."

Her first instinct was to say, *Thanks, but I'm okay.* But that wasn't true. This might be her only chance to find out what lunch at DJ's house would be like. DJ was friendly now, but that could change once this project ended.

"Okay," she said.

They made it to DJ's house ten minutes before his mother pulled into the driveway. Ms. Johnson swept into the house, squeezed DJ's shoulder as she said hello, complimented Nicole on her vibrant choice of earrings, and was more than happy to have Sophia over for lunch.

"As long as your father doesn't mind," she said, handing Sophia the phone.

She stood there in the hallway, the phone pressed against her ear, waiting for her dad to pick up.

DJ popped his head out of the kitchen and mouthed, *Do you like piperade?*

Piperade? Sophia mouthed back at him.

Peppers and tomatoes, DJ said. At least, Sophia was pretty sure that was what he said.

The phone was still ringing, which was weird. Her dad wasn't working today, and he usually hung around the house on his Sundays off, watching TV.

"Yeah, sure," she told DJ. A moment later her house's answering machine came on. She left a quick message, promised to be home in a few hours, and hung up.

The sound of Ms. Johnson's and Nicole's laughter drifted in from the kitchen. It was so infectious that Sophia found herself laughing too, without knowing why.

DJ smiled. "Mom's always in a good mood after book club. She says it's her 'me' time."

"Can you cut onions without crying?" Nicole asked when Sophia and DJ entered the kitchen. She had an onion in each hand, her grip careful, like they were grenades.

"Nicole," Ms. Johnson said, gently scolding, "don't pass off the stuff you don't want to do."

"It's not a matter of *want*," Nicole retorted. "My eyes tear up so bad I'm going to chop my fingers off, I swear."

"I can cut them," Sophia said. "I'll run them under the water while I'm doing it."

With all four of them working—Nicole deigned to wash and slice bell peppers in lieu of the onions—it didn't take long to get everything ready. Piperade was apparently a kind of thick, tomatoey stew.

"Mom likes to cook things from different countries," DJ told Sophia while they searched for eggs in the fridge. "Last month it was the Caribbean. Right now, we're on France."

"The Basque region," Ms. Johnson sang out, and Sophia giggled. She'd never spoken with Ms. Johnson much. She'd always seemed kind of serious, a little *apart* from the other moms and dads milling around. It was strange but nice to see her grinning and comfortable like this.

Even Nicole seemed different, less Rock Star Queen as she made stupid faces at DJ when their mom wasn't looking, kicking her bare feet against the rungs of a stool, resting her chin on their mother's shoulder. Bailey, their big white sheepdog, panted as he jumped about and nipped at everyone's ankles.

It was like the heat of the stove and the close quarters of the kitchen, the communal *chop-chop* of their knives, molded everyone into happier, softer versions of themselves. Or maybe, Sophia thought, that was just the magic of family and home.

Lunch didn't *seem* to take much time, but it was nearly midafternoon by the time the dishwasher was loaded and the leftovers secured in the fridge. DJ showed Sophia his art books. The big, glossy pages featured everything from Michelangelo to pieces by obscure modern artists Sophia didn't recognize. She was flipping through a collection of watercolor portraits when she realized how late it was.

"I guess I should go," she said regretfully, and DJ followed her to the front door, where saying good-bye was suddenly weird and awkward, and neither of them knew where to look, or for how long.

She was relieved to turn away at the end of it, but also a little sad by the time she reached the end of his driveway. Only pride kept her from giving him one last glance over her shoulder. He'd probably already shut the door.

She spent the walk back replaying bits of lunch over and over again in her head, each of them so clear and accompanied by such a rush of feeling that they were almost like Memories.

The house was quiet when she entered.

"Dad?" Sophia called out. His truck had been in the driveway, so she knew he was home.

In the kitchen, the "new message" light flashed on the answering machine; he hadn't checked it yet.

"Dad?" she said, more quietly as she snuck up the stairs.

She edged open his bedroom door. And there he was in bed. He'd been in bed when she'd left this morning. It was midafternoon now, but the blinds were still closed, the room darkened.

"Dad," she said, her heart heavy.

He stirred. Turned to face her. He looked like he hadn't gotten up at all today, and he must have gone to bed in his work shirt last night, because it was all rumpled.

He tried to offer her a smile but didn't quite get there. "Morning."

"It's almost four," Sophia said, then felt bad when his smile disappeared altogether.

"It's been a rough day," he told her.

A queasy weight built in Sophia's stomach. This could be nothing. A blip. A single bad day that would go away tomorrow, and everything would be fine again, the way it had been for months and months now, going on a year.

Or it could be the first of a lot of rough days, the way things had been before. When her dad sleepwalked through hours and days and weeks, barely getting to work, collapsing into bed when he came home.

She'd thought everything was okay. Thought her dad had been okay. Had she missed something? Was it because of what had happened on Thursday? Because she'd gotten upset?

She hadn't meant to screw everything up.

"You hungry?" her dad said. "I think we have left-overs in the fridge."

Sophia shook her head.

Her dad let his head flop back down against the pillows. He took a deep breath, then let it slowly out again.

He looked so, so tired, and she didn't know what to do. How to make it better. The helplessness of it all sat on her chest like an animal.

"Just give me a few more minutes, okay? I'll be up in a bit."

"Okay," Sophia whispered.

She lingered a moment longer by his bed, hoping for—what, she wasn't sure. For him to say something more. For him to smile at her. For him to get out of bed and tell her everything was going to be okay.

He did none of those things.

So she left.

15

AT FIRST SHE JUST WANTED TO GET OUT of the room. Then she just wanted to get down the stairs. Then even that wasn't enough—she had to get out of the house entirely.

Her legs carried her out the front door, across the parched, dying lawn, and down the road.

She still felt strange as she reached the bus stop several blocks down. Like her body wasn't her own, or maybe the world around her—the cracked asphalt, the sun-bleached bus-stop posters, the clouds of lazy gnats—wasn't real.

A pair of girls from her class zoomed by on their bikes. The one in front, Lacey Wilkens, had been in homeroom with Sophia for two years now. Their desks were never far from each other, but she didn't even spare Sophia a glance as she passed.

For some reason, that was the last straw.

She hadn't felt at all like crying until now. She'd been fine until this moment, protected by a haze between her and the rest of the world. By a feeling like she was both here and not here—one foot in her father's darkened bedroom, and another back in DJ's kitchen, chopping onions in the sink.

She cried, and then she stopped crying and wiped her eyes with the heel of her hand.

She should go home. Her dad might have gotten out of bed, and he'd be worried if she wasn't around. It would only stress him out more, and she didn't want that.

They tried so hard, the two of them, to be okay.

She should go home. But she was too sad, too angry, too full of feelings that would only fester at home, where she'd have to hide them.

The bus came. Sophia got onboard and swiped her transit pass, no particular destination in mind.

It was difficult, sometimes, to remember the period right after her mom's death. Everything had been so chaotic. Her mom had been sick for a long time, but as far as Sophia could remember, she'd been doing okay for a few weeks, maybe even a month or two. Then suddenly, she'd gotten worse.

Sophia's grandparents—her mom's parents—had been in town for a while. They'd taken care of everything around the house, been the ones to get Sophia ready for school in the morning and make her dinner at night. Her dad had spent all his time at the hospital.

Then one morning, in the middle of recess, the teacher had found Sophia on the playground and told her that her grandma was here to pick her up. Sophia had been in the middle of a game of King of the Mountain. She'd been King, standing tall on the highest point of the jungle gym, dodging the other kids' attempts to pull her from her perch.

When she saw the teacher coming, she'd thought she'd gotten in trouble. They weren't technically supposed to play King of the Mountain, or stand up on the jungle gym. She'd thought the teacher would yell at her.

Instead she was far too nice. That should have been a clue that something was wrong, but six-year-old Sophia hadn't been as good at reading adults as she was now.

Still, she'd had a bad feeling in the pit of her stomach. A bad feeling that intensified when she saw her grandma in the front office, her eyes red, her hair a mess.

"Oh, darling," she kept saying. "Oh darling, oh darling."

It was like she'd gotten stuck on repeat. Like she couldn't say anything else. She'd grabbed hold of Sophia. Wrapped her arms around her and squeezed her so tight that Sophia couldn't breathe—couldn't find the air to cry, to speak, to do anything at all.

Sophia blinked back to her senses as the bus slowed to a stop. Just about everyone else had disembarked. She looked out the window and yelled, "Wait! I want to get off here!" when the bus driver started moving again.

He slammed on the brakes and sighed at her when she ran past him, down onto the street.

She'd recognized this road. It wasn't far from Donway Shallows.

The abandoned storefronts seemed a lot spookier now than they had earlier, when she'd had DJ and Luke by her side. She hunched her shoulders and walked as quickly as she could.

The woods were even worse. She twitched at every noise, her eyes darting into the underbrush. She kept feeling like she heard distant footsteps—rustling movements just a little bit behind her, or maybe just ahead.

It's probably just more high schoolers, she told herself, and almost believed it. She didn't even think about turning back. She absolutely had to get where she was headed.

To Donway Shallows. To the exact spot she'd been sitting when she'd had the Memory.

She needed another Memory right now. Needed it more than anything.

She rushed past the NO TRESPASSING sign at the edge of the mill, shivering as she struck a sudden patch of cold air. Like before, it came out of nowhere and seemed to have nothing to do with her surroundings.

Sophia had thought Mae was just being weird when she'd claimed the mill had a "special energy," but now she wasn't so sure. There was something strange about the place. It made her feel like she was holding her breath, even when she wasn't.

She slowed as she stepped beneath the mill's cavernous ribs.

"Mae?" she said tentatively.

Something—or someone—clattered in response to

her voice. She froze where she stood, wrapping her arms around herself. "Mae?"

"You," a voice said in surprise. A man's voice. "You—I know you."

Mr. Scot pushed his glasses up his nose as he straightened. He unfolded himself from a dim corner of the mill, rising from the darkness.

"You came to my house," he said. "With Luke."

Sophia nodded warily.

He flapped his hands at her, as if she were a wild critter he could shoo away. He'd rolled up the sleeves of his shirt, and Sophia couldn't help noticing a large bandage on his arm. He hadn't had it yesterday. "It's dangerous here. Didn't you see the No Trespassing sign?"

"Didn't you?" Sophia retorted.

He frowned. "I was just about to leave, in fact."

"Okay," Sophia said. She stepped aside and motioned for him to pass her.

His frown deepened. He didn't move. "You can't stay here by yourself."

"Why not?"

"Because it's dangerous."

Sophia looked around. "I don't see anything dangerous."

He sighed. "Maybe not now, but later. Come on. Did you walk here all by yourself? Where are your parents?"

In bed, she thought.

Gone, she thought.

Mr. Scot came toward her, tried to guide her out of the mill, but Sophia sidestepped out of his way. He limped now. Had he limped before? She was pretty sure he hadn't. "Later? Like during the eclipse?"

He faltered. The twitch was well hidden but perceptible. A rapid blink of his eyes. A thinning of his mouth.

He knew *something*. Something that was a big deal.

Now Sophia was the one pressing into Mr. Scot's space as he tried to scuttle away. "What is it?" she demanded. "What's going to happen? Why are you here? What do you know?"

He shook his head. "It's nothing. It's—"

"I have Memories," Sophia said. She hadn't meant to say it—it burst out of her, a last-ditch attempt at catching his attention, making him take her seriously.

"Memories?" Mr. Scot said.

"Not just normal memories. *Memories*. Memories that I shouldn't have. Things that never happened—like a different version of things. They don't belong. But they're so real, and they're getting more and more real, and there was an eclipse on the day I was born, and my mom, she saw things—she saw me being born before I was actually born—"

She cut off, breathless.

Mr. Scot gave her such a long, flat, dark-eyed look that she quailed. She didn't know what that look meant. What he was thinking. If she'd made some mistake in telling him these things.

"How long have you been having these Memories?" he asked.

Sophia took a deep breath. She had to be brave, to take chances. She'd never get anything she wanted otherwise. "Since my mother died."

"Ah," he said.

Everything that he'd said or done before this moment hadn't made a dent in Sophia's determination, her bull-headed belief that anything was still possible—that Mr. Scot might be able to help her, if only Sophia could convince him to do it.

But the look on his face now as he spoke that single word stole all the wind from Sophia's sails.

It was the same look she'd seen on Nurse Loi's face.

On the faces of the guidance counselors she'd seen over the years. On the faces of random adults around town, people who'd known her mother, known how their family had been once upon a time, before everything fell apart.

Pity.

It was not a look she wanted to see on anyone, at any time. But especially not now.

Mr. Scot wasn't supposed to pity her. Wasn't supposed to look at her like this, like Sophia was some poor lost cause. He was supposed to *help* her.

"Don't you need to get home for dinner?" he said.

Sophia shoved her fury down before it could grow. Buried it deep with all the other small angers in her life, where she didn't have to look at them, and they couldn't hurt her.

"No, I'm staying right here," she said.

Mr. Scot looked around helplessly, as if he hoped she might change her mind. Sophia stared right back at him every time he met her eyes.

He sighed. "All right. If you come back to my car with me, and let me take you home, I'll answer your questions."

Sophia considered this. Mr. Scot seemed nice

enough, if aloof. But there was something strange about him, some unsolved riddle in his mysterious research, his sudden injuries. And Sophia's trust didn't come easy. "I'll go back to the main road with you. But I'm taking the bus home."

"Fine, fine." Mr. Scot threw up his hands. "You do what you like. As long as you head home."

Sophia nodded. He nodded back.

She waited for him to move first, then followed him out of the mill.

16

MR. SCOT WAS A FAST WALKER. OR MAYBE
he was just trying to reach his car as quickly as possible,
so Sophia wouldn't have time to ask too many questions.

"Well?" she demanded as Donway Shallows faded out
of view behind them.

"Well what?"

"You promised you'd answer my questions."

"And what are your questions?"

Sophia huffed. She wasn't a slow walker herself, but
her legs were a lot shorter than Mr. Scot's. There was
only so much ground she could cover per stride.

"What's so special about that mill?" she said. "What does
it have to do with the solar eclipse? And my Memories?"

Mr. Scot waited so long to answer that Sophia was afraid he wouldn't. Finally he said, "What do you know about déjà vu?"

"It's a feeling you get. A feeling that something's already happened before."

Mr. Scot nodded. "Is that all?"

"Yeah, that's what the words mean," Sophia said, frustrated. Couldn't he just be forthright? "It's just a weird feeling."

"So what your mother experienced on the day you were born—you think that was just a weird feeling as well?"

Sophia shook her head. "No, it was more than that. It wasn't just déjà vu. She *saw* me being born."

Mr. Scot shrugged.

"It wasn't just déjà vu," Sophia said fiercely.

"I don't know if déjà vu is 'just' anything," Mr. Scot mused. "Why do you think you feel it? Or other people feel it? Don't you think it's strange, being struck by the feeling that something has already happened? Why would you feel that way? Why only sometimes?"

Sophia stared at him, waiting for an answer. When it didn't come, she bit back a sigh. "I don't know."

Mr. Scot waited. They were getting too close to the main road for Sophia's comfort. She still had so much to ask.

"Because it did happen," she said, just to say something, to get him talking again. "You feel like it already happened because it *did* already happen."

He raised his eyebrows. "How could that be? How could something happen twice?"

Sophia was starting to feel like she was back in school, taking a test on something she'd never learned. *I don't know,* she almost said again, but that hadn't done her much good the first time.

"Things being on a loop?" she said. "Or, like . . ."

She thought back, suddenly, to the notebook on Mr. Scot's armchair. To the handwritten lettering on the cover: *The Universes, This One and Beyond.*

"Like a parallel universe," she said.

"Now *there's* an idea," said Mr. Scot. His eyebrows rose approvingly, and he tilted his head, as if studying Sophia in a new light. "What if, every time you had déjà vu, it wasn't just a trick of the mind, but a momentary . . . thinning of the film between worlds? You feel like something's already happened because in that other world, it did." He snapped his fingers. "And there you go: déjà vu."

Sophia's heartbeat crescendoed. "And my Memories? Are they the same thing? Me brushing against another world?"

"Perhaps," said Mr. Scot. He'd fallen into a rhythm as he talked. He sounded a bit like Mr. Rae when he rambled about a book he loved. "There are many ways thoughts and memories could swish between worlds, I suppose. People who feel that they don't belong somewhere, for example, might be feeling the disconnect between the place they're living and where they live in another version of the world. Or musicians who claim a piece of music floated right out of their minds in a fever—they might have just nabbed it from their crisscrossed memories of another life, where they've already composed the piece."

"How come it happens to some people and not others?" Sophia said. "Why me? Why my mom? And—"

And DJ, and Ms. Johnson, she almost added, but cut herself off. Those weren't her secrets to share.

"Do you think it's genetic?" she asked instead.

"It could be. Or it could have something to do with where you grew up, or the state of the universes when you were born, or—" He hesitated. "Or it might be the loss you've suffered. If you want something badly enough, something you don't have here, it could affect your sensitivity for other worlds."

He glanced down at Sophia and cleared his throat. "Anyway, it wouldn't surprise me if children were more sensitive to this sort of thing overall. Adults have too much other junk in their heads already. They make for crowded receivers. An idea or a memory might cross, but bounce right off."

"What about people?" Sophia said. "Can people cross worlds?"

Something must have shone through in her voice— some inkling of her longing—because the scientist gave her a sad, quiet look.

"Ah," he said, "here's my car."

"What?" Sophia said.

Mr. Scot gestured to the beat-up sedan parked ahead. Sophia had been too engrossed in their conversation to notice they'd left the woods.

"Are you sure you wouldn't like a ride?" he said. "I'll at least take you to the bus stop."

"Can people cross worlds?" said Sophia insistently.

Mr. Scot stopped walking and regarded her.

"No," he said. "I've never heard of such a thing."

Something crumpled in Sophia's chest. It might have been her lungs. Or something delicate but essential in her heart.

He took his keys from his pocket and fiddled with them in his hand while Sophia stood there silently. Minutes passed, one by one.

"Ride?" he offered again.

Sophia shook her head.

Sophia's dad was still asleep when she got home. She tiptoed to his bedroom door—the bedroom he'd shared with her mother once upon a time—and peeked inside, just to make sure. His breathing stayed deep and slow. He was out.

She waited one, two, three seconds, in case her presence woke him. It didn't.

She warmed up spaghetti from the fridge and ate it by herself at the kitchen counter. Then she crept upstairs into bed.

"I miss her too," she said into the silence of her house.

17

SOPHIA WOKE TO THE SMELL OF PANCAKES.

"Good morning, sleepy," her dad said as she padded into the kitchen, barefoot and rubbing dreams from her eyes. He slipped another steaming pancake onto a plate before untying his apron and switching off the stove. "You hungry?"

Sophia fought the urge to stare at him. Part of her wondered if she was still asleep. Her dad had a morning shift at Tom's today. He wasn't even supposed to still be home, let alone making her breakfast.

"Aren't you late for work?" she said.

He pressed a kiss against her forehead as he pushed the plate of pancakes into her hands. They were blueberry and walnut, her favorite since she'd been a little girl. Her mother had made them for her on special occasions—birthdays, Christmases, first days of spring.

"I gave them a heads-up already." Her dad's voice was low, raspy like he was sick. There were bags under his eyes. He hadn't ironed his shirt—Tom would be upset about that. But he was out of bed, and he'd made Sophia pancakes. She wasn't sure how to feel. "I wanted to say good morning before I left."

"Oh." Sophia looked down at the pancakes. They smelled like heaven and felt like an apology. He'd only made enough for her. "Good morning."

He gave her a quick smile before reaching for his keys. Despite what he'd said about giving Tom a heads-up, he'd already put on his shoes. "You sleep all right?"

He didn't bring up yesterday afternoon. Sophia hadn't expected him to. This was the way things were. Rough days weren't talked about. Unhappy things weren't talked about. They, like the death of Sophia's mother, were wounds that never healed properly, and hurt too much to touch.

She shrugged. "I slept okay."

"How's the project going? You were working on it this weekend, right?"

"It's going okay."

"Good, good," he said. "Do you want to do something fun together next Saturday? I'm off the whole day. We can go to the movies, or hang out at the park. Anywhere you want."

"Okay," Sophia said.

"Great," he said. He didn't seem to know what else to say. "Well, you have a good day at—"

"Dad?"

He'd already turned toward the door, but he twisted back to smile at her. "Yeah, Sophia?"

Sophia swallowed. Over the years, she'd gotten used to her father's near silence about her mother. She'd come to feel as apprehensive about mentioning her as he was. Just the thought of bringing her up made Sophia's throat close up, her chest hurt.

But she wanted to, so badly. The Memories could only give her so much. They didn't tell her what her mother's favorite foods had been, or what she'd been like when she was Sophia's age.

They didn't let Sophia know if her mother had said

anything special about her before she died. If she'd known it was coming.

If she'd wanted to see Sophia one last time, and hadn't gotten the chance.

"Sophia?" He was starting to look worried, and Sophia hated to be one more thing he worried about.

"Never mind," she said softly, and went to kiss him on the cheek.

Sophia and DJ took the bus to Luke's house again after school, to work on their eclipse project. Of course, there was their eclipse project for Mr. Rae, and then there was their Eclipse Project. The one that involved the Memories, and Donway Shallows, and the mystery that was Mr. Scot.

Luke's father met them at the door, exhaustingly cheerful and questioning—had they had a good day? What had they learned about? Were they going to stay for dinner? Did they need to call their parents? Were they sure?

Luke dodged his father like a professional athlete, but that meant the brunt of it fell to Sophia and DJ. They did the best they could, smiling and chatting until Luke secured some snacks and ushered them upstairs to his room.

He shut the door with visible embarrassment and relief. "It wasn't like this when Marni was alive."

It was the first time he'd ever brought up his sister. Neither Sophia nor DJ knew how to respond.

"Sorry," DJ said finally. "About your sister, I mean. That sucks."

Luke nodded without looking at them.

"So," Sophia said, when the quiet had gone on too long, and she didn't know what else to say. "The eclipse is in four days."

DJ nodded. "And our project is due in two. Did you write up your bit about the Pomo myths? We can add it to the rest of the paper. After that, it's mostly the conclusion, I guess."

Sophia had not written up her bit about the Pomo myths. She hadn't even thought about Mr. Rae's project over the weekend. How could she, when there was something so much bigger at stake?

She'd already caught DJ and Luke up on everything Mr. Scot had told her. And frankly, she'd expected this meeting to have very little to do with their research paper.

Some of her disappointment must have bled into her expression, because DJ said, "We can still talk about the other stuff. But we're going to have to turn this in on Wednesday, so it would be nice to have it done."

Who cares if it's done? Sophia wanted to snap. How could he think about schoolwork when they should be considering *parallel universes?*

He just didn't get it.

He had the Memories, and the dream of a different life—but it wasn't the same. How could it be, when this life still blessed him with a mom who cooked meals from around the world, and a big sister who drove him places, and a house that closed around him like an embrace?

Sophia's dad had been all right this morning. But she didn't know which version of him she'd find when she went home. The one who'd driven her three hours on his one day off to go paddleboating at the state park? Or the one who couldn't get out of bed, couldn't open the blinds, at three in the afternoon?

Things were better now. A lot better.

But some days still hurt in a way that DJ couldn't know.

If he did, he wouldn't be talking about school projects.

"Hey," DJ said, studying her. "You okay?"

Sophia flushed. She had too many emotions again, and nowhere to put them.

"I'll write my part after I get home," she said. "I swear. But the eclipse is Friday, DJ. What if—"

Sophia had told DJ and Luke everything about her conversation with Mr. Scot—everything but the very last question she'd asked him: *Can people cross worlds?*

If she didn't tell them she'd asked, she didn't have to tell them his answer.

She took a deep breath. "If there's actually a way to make our Memories real, for us to make it so that my mom's still alive—that your mom really did meet your stepdad— If there's any way we could do it, I bet it would have something to do with the eclipse. With this Friday. We have to figure it out before then, DJ. We can't miss our chance."

DJ stared down at Luke's carpet, frowning. Sophia wished she could see inside his brain.

"What about me?" Luke said softly.

He'd been so quiet that Sophia had almost forgotten he was there. Luke's eyes flickered from DJ to Sophia. His freckles sat in bleak constellations across his pale cheeks.

"I've never had a Memory," he said. "Not like yours. Do you think that means it won't work for me? Do you think I'll get Marni back?"

It wasn't a question Sophia could answer. She didn't even know if crossing was possible at all, for anyone. Certainly, Mr. Scot hadn't thought so.

"I don't think it should matter," she said slowly. "Mr. Scot said I might have the Memories just because I was born at the right time, or in the right place. Or because I—well, because I *want* something so badly. You were born in the same hospital, even if it was a different day. And—"

"And I want Marni back," Luke said fiercely. "I want my parents to be the way they were before. I want everything to be the way it was before. That should be enough, don't you think?"

It didn't really matter what Sophia thought. Only what Luke needed to hear right now.

"I think you have a chance," she told him. "I think you have as good a chance as anyone."

Luke nodded, seemingly convinced. Or at least willing to be convinced. DJ shot Sophia a look she couldn't decipher.

She climbed to her feet and noted with satisfaction that Luke was doing the same. "Are we going to do this or not?"

"Yes," Luke said.

Sophia nodded. Waited.

"Okay," DJ said. But he didn't smile, and the knot in Sophia's chest didn't ease.

"What're we going to do?" Luke asked. "Should we go find Mr. Scot again?"

Sophia shook her head. "I don't think he'd tell us anything more. Not unless we had some way of forcing him. Like, blackmail or something."

"I'm pretty sure he's too boring to blackmail," Luke said. "He doesn't leave his house much. He says the world is out to get him."

"I don't think we should be blackmailing people at all," said DJ.

Sophia ignored them both. If they didn't go back to Mr. Scot, where else would they go? Who else would give them information?

She closed her eyes and tried to remember the layout of Mr. Scot's study, to remember the books he'd had scattered across the floor.

All that came to mind was the portrait he'd hung on the wall. The woman playing the cello, her face hidden in shadow, her fingers delicate on her bow.

And the newspaper clipping.

Of course. Why hadn't she thought of that earlier?

"'The Mystery of Donway Shallows,'" she said.

"You were just there," Luke said. "You think you're going to find something new?"

Sophia shook her head. "No—I mean, maybe. But that's not what I meant. We need to find the newspaper that clipping came from. I bet there are archives somewhere. Whatever was in that article, it was important enough for Mr. Scot to save."

"The library keeps records of newspapers." DJ shrugged. "Maybe they'd have a copy."

"Library it is, then," said Sophia.

18

IN ADDITION TO HER MEMORIES, SOPHIA
possessed a small but precious bouquet of normal,
lowercase memories of her mother. Many of them took
place here, at the public library. Her mom had worked
various jobs—waitress, movie theater attendant, per-
fume seller. But every summer, she'd spent Saturdays
at the library.

Sophia wasn't sure what her job had been. Something
involving the front desk. She hadn't cared back then—
she'd just liked coming with her mom to work. They'd
walk up to the library door, Sophia holding her mom's
hand. She'd loved the automatic doors. Loved the way
she and her mom said *Swish!* together when they opened.

It was Sophia's job to pick out three books while her mom worked. Two books for her to take home and bring back next Saturday. One book for her and her mom to read right after work, the two of them curled up in the pile of beanbags at the edge of the children's area.

Two years after Sophia's mother died, the library revamped the children's area. They replaced the bean-bags—which all leaked beans—with brightly colored armchairs.

By then, Sophia rarely came to the library anymore. It took more than half an hour by bus—sometimes even longer, when the buses came late—and it just hadn't been the same.

Swish, she thought as she stepped through the library's automatic doors.

Luke's dad had been more than happy to drive them to the library, but he now seemed prepared to stay here until they were ready to leave. He drifted toward a collection of magazines by the checkout desk but glanced up from time to time to see what Sophia and the boys were doing.

Luke refused to look at him as they walked past, but

Sophia gave him a little wave. Hopefully, he'd stay put while they searched for the Donway Shallows article.

"We're looking for a copy of an old newspaper," DJ said to the woman at the information desk.

She smiled. "Sure thing. How old are we talking?"

DJ looked at Sophia, who scrunched up her face in thought, then shrugged. She didn't remember a date on the newspaper clipping. It had definitely been hanging on that corkboard for a while, though. Long enough for the print to have faded, and the edges to have gone soft.

"Kind of old?" she said.

"Okay," the librarian said, "maybe we'd have it on microfilm, then. Shall we go check?"

Sophia had no idea what microfilm was, but she nodded.

The woman led them to a little room toward the back of the library and motioned for them to sit while she unlocked a silver filing cabinet. Inside sat rows and rows of white boxes. Each bore a handwritten label.

The librarian gestured to a funny-looking machine on the table. It had an old-timey-looking film reel on one end and was connected to a computer on the other end.

"You guys ever use one of these?" she asked.

Sophia looked at DJ and Luke, but neither of them volunteered an answer, so she shook her head.

"It's not hard," the librarian said. "But I'll help you guys out. Now, do you have any more clues about this newspaper you're looking for? Was it local or national?"

"I'm not sure," Sophia said.

"Well, we're going to need something to narrow it down." The librarian tapped the file cabinet with one long, manicured nail. "Otherwise, you're going to be going through a whole lot of microfilm."

"The article was called 'The Mystery of Donway Shallows,'" Sophia said.

The librarian gave a surprised laugh. "That old textile mill? Well, I very much doubt anything but a local paper would write about that place. How about we start with this box, then?"

She opened one of the white cardboard boxes to reveal a big reel of film. Sophia watched carefully as she threaded it onto the machine. After a minute or two of fiddling, a grainy scan of the *Hillside Gazette* popped up on the computer screen. It was dated about five years ago.

"You can press these buttons to scroll through the

editions," the librarian said. "I'm going to head back to my desk, but come get me if you want to put in another reel."

Sophia took the seat in front of the computer, the boys flanking her The first three newspapers were pretty cool to look through. Sophia scrutinized each headline. By the fifth, the excitement had faded. By the eighth, it was gone entirely.

DJ fetched the librarian to change the reel.

"No luck?" the woman asked.

"Nope," Sophia said. She hadn't really thought about how many papers the *Hillside Gazette* had put out in just the last year. And how many years were they going to check? Five years? Ten? Fifteen?

Sophia's neck hurt by the end of the third reel. Her eyes hurt by the end of the fifth.

The librarian gave up coming in every time to change the reel. She supervised DJ once carefully, to make sure he knew how to do it, then gave him the go-ahead to change the rest himself.

Neither of the boys said anything, but Sophia felt the weight of each passing minute. There was a whole cabinet full of *Hillside Gazette* reels. Looking through them all would take the rest of the night.

They worked their way through five more reels. Then ten.

A knock came at the door. Luke's dad poked his head in.

"You kids about ready to head out?" he said.

Luke shook his head. "Not yet. We haven't found what we're looking for."

"And what are you looking for?" His dad stepped toward them, and Sophia fought the urge to cover up the computer screen. The last thing she wanted was Luke's dad getting in the middle of their search.

"Stuff for our project, Dad." Luke stood, as if to usher his dad back out of the room. "We need more time."

His dad beckoned him over. Luke heaved a sigh and went. They kept their voices low, but Sophia caught the gist of their conversation: Luke's dad saying that it was getting late, that they needed to get home for dinner, Luke protesting that this was important, that dinner could wait.

"Wait!" DJ whispered. "Stop—go back a page."

Distracted by the conversation behind her, and tired after more than an hour of clicking through newspapers, Sophia had barely glanced at the last page before clicking next. She backed up.

"There." DJ pointed. "There it is!"

19

SOPHIA'S HEARTBEAT QUICKENED. BOTH of them scooted forward in their chairs. It wasn't a long article, just a few skinny paragraphs squished beside the margin.

The Mystery of Donway Shallows

For decades, Donway Shallows has stood abandoned in the historic district. Once a vital part of town industry, it now serves as a relic of days gone by, visited only by vandals and the odd drunken teenage party.

Last week, it served as the setting for yet another noteworthy town event. When

"I have to go home," Luke said.

Sophia nearly jumped out of her skin. "But we just found it," she told him. She tapped on the computer screen. "Look—"

"I know," Luke said miserably. "But I have to go home. My dad's asking if you guys need a ride back too."

DJ shook his head. "We can take the bus."

Luke lingered another moment by their chairs, his mouth a harsh, unhappy line.

"Can't you convince him to let you stay?" Sophia whispered. "You could take the bus with us. Or just come to my place for dinner."

Luke snorted. "He'd never be okay with that. Not before meeting your dad in person and asking him a million questions and scouting out your house first. Plus, we always have to have dinner together as a family now. Every night."

"Luke?" his father said.

Luke sighed. "Tell me everything you find out," he said, and waited for them to both swear it before he followed his dad from the room.

Sophia swiveled around to read the rest of the article. It was so short, and she was so excited, that she had to read it twice before any of the words stuck in her head. By the end of the second read, she'd gleaned the most pertinent facts:

1. This article had been written thirteen years ago, about a week after Sophia's birth

2. The "noteworthy town event" it was talking about had happened on June 11

3. Which *was* Sophia's birthday

4. The "event" itself was foggy, because it had occurred early in the morning, and the only witness had been an old gentleman who frequented the area

5. Said man was very advanced in age and had only been able to give an addled account of things

6. First he said it had been a man

7. Then he said it had been a woman

8. But one thing remained constant

9. He was very, very sure that as he passed through Donway Shallows that morning, he saw a person appear where, a moment before, no person had stood

"DJ," Sophia breathed. "It's possible. People can cross."

"Hold on," DJ said. "This is barely anything—this

is like three paragraphs about something a guy *maybe* saw—"

"This happened on my—on our birthday," Sophia said. "Exactly on the same day, the day of the last eclipse. And Mr. Scot didn't just have it on his wall for nothing. You saw all those books in his study. He's been looking into Donway Shallows and eclipses a lot longer than we have. He wouldn't still be poking around the mill if he thought it was 'barely anything.'"

DJ opened his mouth to reply, but Sophia barreled onward. "We just have to figure out who this person was—this person the old man saw."

"They're probably not around anymore." DJ's voice, unlike Sophia's, got quieter instead of louder. "If they're even real."

Sophia turned away from him and spoke at the computer screen. "It was real enough to write an article about. Look, it says the mysterious figure was slim, and they seemed really out of it—kept muttering to themselves . . . saying Donway Shallows was a special place—"

"I don't know if we can trust that," DJ said. "Who did they interview? The witness couldn't even say if it was a man or a woman—how do we know he actually remembered anything about them, or what they said?"

"Well, they were right about it being a special place," Sophia muttered. "Even Mae—"

A thought struck her, slammed into her so hard that it knocked all other thoughts and emotions right out of her head.

"The crosser," she breathed. "What if it's Mae?"

"Sophia." DJ didn't sound the way she wanted him to sound—shocked and pleased and excited. He sounded like he was going to be boring and discouraging again, and Sophia couldn't take that right now.

She had her next clue. She had her next thread, and maybe it wasn't the strongest of leads, maybe it was thin and a little bit nebulous, but she could work with that.

Sophia was used to things in her life not being a hundred percent. Her mom not being a hundred percent. Her dad not being a hundred percent.

She just needed something to work with. Something to hold on to.

She stood and shut off the computer. "I'm going to find her."

"Who, Mae?" DJ said. "Now?"

Sophia nodded. Her mind buzzed as she put the

boxes of reels back into the filing cabinet. She'd go to the bus stop near the hospital first, since that was closer. If Mae wasn't there, she'd try Donway Shallows next.

"I don't know if this is a good idea," DJ said slowly. "You can't—you're not just going to ask her if she's from another universe. Are you?"

"I'll figure it out," Sophia said.

She grabbed her book bag and headed for the door. DJ fiddled around with the computer for another few seconds, then rushed to catch up.

"She's got enough people bothering her," he warned Sophia. "You're just going to offend her if you show up telling her you think she doesn't belong."

Sophia hated how bossy he sounded. Hated, too, that he might be talking sense.

"I'll be nice," she promised as they exited the library. "She won't think I'm bothering her."

DJ had caught up so they were walking side by side. He hesitated as she set off across the library's parking lot, and she slowed too. They regarded each other across the baking concrete.

The sun glared over DJ's shoulder, making Sophia squint.

"Are you going to come?" she said finally.

DJ looked back at the library, then out to the bus stop at the bottom of the hill. He scrutinized his shoes.

"Yeah, okay," he said.

Sophia was surprised by her own relief. She'd never been the sort to need other people to do stuff with her. But going to visit Mae with DJ would be like going to the hospital with DJ, or exploring Donway Shallows for the first time with DJ.

Just better.

20

THE BUS GROANED TO A STOP BY THE

hospital.

Sophia's stomach twisted. The bus shelter was empty but for two teenagers. No Mae.

She and DJ got off the bus anyway. It was evening, but still hot. Maybe Mae would come once the air cooled.

The two of them squeezed onto the far end of the bus shelter bench, away from the teenagers and their cloud of cigarette smoke. They watched the horizon for Mae sightings, swatting futilely at clouds of dusk-hunting gnats.

A bus came. Then another. It was after-work hours now; the stop filled with and then emptied of waves of passengers—office workers in their wilted collars and scratched-up briefcases, waitresses nursing aching feet and counting tips.

The teenagers stomped out their cigarettes before boarding. DJ pulled out his sketchbook and doodled, glancing up only when they heard footsteps. He and Sophia hadn't spoken on the bus, and they didn't speak now. There was something unrepaired between them, and the jagged edges of it scared them both.

DJ was braver than she was, because he spoke first.

"I do care," he said, then added rapidly, "About the project. What we're doing here. With the eclipse and Donway Shallows and everything."

He tugged at his shirt, the way he did when he was uncomfortable.

It hadn't been very long since he and Sophia had gone from strangers to friends. She was surprised by how well she understood the meaning behind his fidgeting, the way he looked at her, then away from her, then back again.

"My mom—she wasn't happy with my dad. I mean, I guess she was once upon a time. They were married and all, and they had Nicole, and they had me, and he—well, he stuck around until the last bit." He made a face, and laughed. "I guess I was a really terrible baby."

"All babies are terrible," Sophia said. "I'm sure you were fine. I bet you didn't even cry that much."

"Nicole says I cried nonstop. But she might be making that up. She also says Mom and Dad started fighting around then."

Sophia considered this. Then considered, slowly, the best response she could give. She decided, in the end, on the truth.

"That doesn't mean it was your fault."

"Oh, I know," DJ said, too casually.

"Have you ever met him?" she asked.

He nodded. "A few times, yeah. More when I was younger. Not since fifth grade. He lives four hours away now. And . . . it was always sort of weird whenever we did meet. Like he didn't know what to do with me, and to be honest, I didn't really know what to do with him, either. He's my *dad*, you know? But he's not the way . . . the way dads are supposed to be, I think. I don't know. Is there a way dads are supposed to be?"

That wasn't a question Sophia could answer. DJ gave her a faint smile.

"If there is, I think it's the way my stepdad is. In my Memories." His smile widened. "He's great, Sophia. He's really, really great. I wish you could meet him. I wish my mom could meet him. I mean, the way she has in the Memories. He makes her so happy. They're all cute and embarrassing. It's a bit awkward, honestly."

He laughed and looked away.

Sophia found herself giggling too. DJ looked at her in surprise. The tension between them cracked and broke away.

"I want that," DJ said. "For me. For her. For Nicole."

"I know," Sophia said.

He took a deep breath and nodded. It was all they needed to say about the matter. Everything else was understood.

The sun lowered, and the gnats grew more ferocious. DJ finished up his drawing, which turned out to be a portrait of Sophia.

She flushed when she looked at it, even though it was a perfectly non-embarrassing picture. If anything, it showed her looking pretty boring, sitting there slouched on the bench, her hair messy, her shirt too big, her legs stick-skinny beneath her shorts. DJ seemed pleased with it, though, so she tried to be enthusiastic for his sake. It was an *accurate* portrayal, at any rate, even if she didn't look particularly nice in it.

Something flashed in the corner of her vision. She straightened. "Hey, that's her, isn't it?"

The figure was still two blocks away, so it was hard to be sure. Sophia jumped to her feet, squinting as it meandered closer, became a tiny old lady who walked with her shoulders hunched, her head bent toward her dog. Even from this distance, Sophia could tell she was chattering to the animal.

Soon, she picked up snippets of the conversation—comments about the bathtub-warm air, the never-ending swarm of gnats, the chicken sandwich they'd had for dinner.

"Mae!" Sophia called out.

The woman looked up. For a few seconds, she didn't seem to recognize the girl waving at her. Her shoulders went stiff, her jaw tight. Then she got closer, and her body unwound again.

"Ah, it's you," she said. "Where's the other boy? The pale, frowny one?"

"He had to go home for dinner," Sophia said.

Mae nodded. "And what about you two? Don't you need your dinners?"

"We need to ask you something," Sophia said. Mae's dog was snuffing around Sophia's shoes again, and she resisted the urge to nervously back away.

Mae raised her eyebrows, waiting. Sophia hesitated. She'd promised DJ that she'd ask Mae without offending her, and she intended to keep that promise.

"We're trying to learn about parallel universes," Sophia said.

Mae's eyebrows climbed even higher. "Parallel universes?"

"Some people think you can, you know, travel from one universe to another."

"Do they now?" Mae laughed. "Well, that's the stupidest thing I've ever heard."

Sophia wasn't sure how she'd expected this to play out—how she'd expected Mae to respond when she asked her about parallel universes. But she'd wanted more than *this*.

She'd dragged DJ here. They'd waited forever at the bus stop.

She hadn't done all that just so Mae could laugh in her face.

Sophia swallowed. She'd promised she wouldn't upset Mae with her questions, but now *she* was the one getting upset.

"There was an article on it," she said, as calmly as she could. "About Donway Shallows, and—"

"Here." DJ held out his phone. He must have taken a picture of the article when Sophia wasn't paying attention. She gave him a thankful look while Mae scrolled through the article.

"This is ancient news," she said. "Why're you kids—"

Her expression fluttered, then shifted. She studied the article a moment longer, then looked up at Sophia.

"Ah," she said. It was a weighty word. "Are you trying to ask if that was me?"

No, Sophia almost said, but Mae had the sort of eyes that saw through lies, and she couldn't manage to spit the word out.

She didn't say *yes*, either, but her face said it for her.

"Was it?" she asked.

Mae snorted. "Say it was. So what?"

"We want to know how you did it," Sophia said.

Mae laughed again. "Is this world really so bad, you gotta leave it for another one?" She bent to ruffle her dog's fur as he panted in the heat. "Sure, not everything turns out the way you'd want. But it is the way it is."

"It could be better," Sophia said.

Mae made a *hmmmph* noise in the back of her throat. "Perhaps. Have you thought about what'll happen *here*, if you do cross?"

Sophia hadn't thought about *here*, only *there*. Only about where she wanted to go.

"Say it all works—you do whatever you're going to do and end up in the worlds you want to be in." Mae gestured with her hands. "Are you just going to switch bodies with the versions of you that were already there? Are those versions of you going to come here, to this universe? Are you just going to leave a hole behind?"

Sophia had no answers for any of that.

Behind them, the next bus pulled up, the doors whooshing open. A handful of people spilled into the evening heat. None of them paid any attention to the old woman and kids on the corner.

"You think we shouldn't do it?" DJ said. "Even if we could?"

Mae shook her head. "What do I know? I'm just a crazy old lady."

Sophia didn't know what to think. Not anymore. She'd tried so hard to keep herself from wavering, no matter what. But now that was falling apart, and she could see the edges of other things crumbling too—all the hopes she'd hinged on Mae being the crosser.

What now?

"We should go," DJ said to Mae. He tugged gently on Sophia's wrist. "Sorry for bothering you."

Mae nodded. Sophia let DJ guide her back toward the bench. She was too upset to speak. This whole trip had been a waste. Maybe all that time spent looking through newspapers at the library had been a waste too. Because what did they have now?

DJ had been right, and she'd been stupid not to listen. Stupid to think that a silly article written thirteen years ago would be the final piece in the puzzle. The ticket to everything she wanted.

She squeezed her eyes shut.

Fought against the roaring in her ears.

And nearly cried with relief when the Memory hit.

21

IT TOOK HER A MOMENT TO REALIZE
where the Memory had whisked her, because it looked
so different.

It was her own living room. Except the couches were
dark blue, and there were two of them—not the solitary
lumpy gray one that usually sat in Sophia's living room.
The goofy pictures of her dad and her above the fire-
place were gone, replaced by a funny-looking clock and
some wooden knickknacks. Paintings Sophia didn't recognize hung on the walls: prints of pouncing foxes and
sad-eyed deer.

What's wrong? someone said. Or sort of said. Spoken

words were always strange in Memories—more like suggestions of sound than actual voices.

In the Memory, Sophia turned. She sat on one of the blue couches. There was a frayed, eggshell-colored pillow tucked against her, like she was hugging it to herself. She got the impression that she was sad, though she wasn't sure why.

Her mother, curled beside her, said, *Sophie, did something happen at school again?*

No one ever called Sophia *Sophie* except her mother. Or at least she did in the Memories.

Her mother looked worried. Sophia ached to tell her about the frustrating conversation she'd just had with Mae. About the way she couldn't stop worrying about her father. About the Memories, and the solar eclipse, and how Sophia was going to cross universes if that's what it took to find her.

About everything, basically.

It'll be all right, darling, her mother said. *You can't always be friends with everyone.*

She smiled and squeezed Sophia's hands. *Just be kind to them, Sophie. Be as kind and as understanding as you can. It's all anyone can ask.*

The Memory receded gently, leaving Sophia with a quiet sort of peace.

It'll be all right, her mother had said.

Maybe that was all it had taken to make Sophia calm down: a mother to assure her that things would be all right.

She must not have been out of it for very long, because Mae was still shuffling away from them, her head bent to chat with her dog. It was a scene Sophia had seen all her life: Mae and her dog. And yet—

"Be right back," she said to DJ.

She ran to catch up with Mae. "What's your last name?"

The old woman blinked in surprise. Of all the questions Sophia could have asked, she seemed to have expected this one least. It startled her even more than Sophia's probing about parallel universes.

"My last name? What do you want that for?"

She sounded so defensive that Sophia felt a pang of guilt. When was the last time someone had asked Mae anything about herself? Even for something as simple as her full name? "I just—I realized I don't know it. And I want to."

Mae gave her a searching look, as if she didn't trust Sophia's sudden interest. Didn't trust that she actually cared.

"My full name is Anna-Mae Kent," she said finally.

"Okay." Sophia stuck out her hand. Solemnly, Mae took it. Her fingers were thin, but strong.

"Nice to meet you," said Sophia.

"Likewise," said Mae.

Sophia turned to head back to DJ. She got about two steps away before Mae's hand closed on her shoulder.

"Wait," the woman said. "I guess I just remembered. I do have something else to tell you about parallel universes."

DJ must have realized that something was happening, because he'd left the bench and was hurrying toward them.

"It's not much," Mae warned. "It's just a story I've heard."

"Tell me," Sophia said. "Please."

Mae beckoned her and DJ off the sidewalk. They followed her to a sunny patch of grass, which she sank down onto with a happy sigh.

"My back, you know," she told Sophia, then laughed

and said, "I suppose you don't. But you will one day."

Sophia had zero interest in her future back pains, but she nodded as patiently as she could.

"The story?" she prompted.

Mae nodded. "I can't even remember where I heard it anymore. Was it Louise? Yes, Louise was always into this sort of thing—the occult, and spirits, and crystals. Oh, that woman loved her crystals."

Sophia bit her lip to keep from hurrying Mae along. The last thing she wanted to do was offend her, or make her clam up again.

"Anyway," Mae said. "The point is, Louise was like you. There were things she wanted that she couldn't get in this world, so she was always looking for other options. Sometimes that was the afterlife. Sometimes it was communing with the trees. And sometimes, it was parallel universes."

She gave Sophia and DJ a meaningful look. "Personally, I think Louise was a little too eager to believe. She became convinced that parallel universes were not only real, but reachable. That somewhere out there were worlds where her life was entirely different—entirely better—and if she just did the right things, followed the right steps"—Mae waved her hands about—"said the right magic words, then she could cross over and live there."

She paused, her eyebrows furrowed in thought. "I can't promise I'm going to tell this next part right. It was so long ago, and to be honest, sometimes I only half listened to Louise when she went into one of her rants about this stuff."

"That's okay," DJ said. "What do you remember?"

"First she had to find a place where the barrier between worlds was thinnest," Mae said. "That's how I got pulled into this whole thing, you know. Because I was the one who told her about Donway Shallows, and how special it felt."

"And then?" Sophia said, when Mae paused yet again.

"She needed something to guide her to the right world," Mae said. "Talismans or tokens that connected her to where she wanted to go. I can't remember what she picked. Like I said, it was so long ago."

Sophia exchanged a glance with DJ. He looked as uncertain as she felt. Could they trust Mae's story? Mae barely seemed to trust her own story.

"What happened after that?" DJ pressed. "Where's Louise now?"

Mae shrugged. "She went away."

"Away?" Sophia said. "Away where?"

Jimmy whined as he discovered an abandoned choc-
olate bar wrapper just beyond his reach. Mae shifted
to allow him more leash. "Difficult to say. Sometimes
people just come and go, you know?"

"Didn't you wonder about it?" Sophia asked. "Weren't
you worried when she disappeared?"

As someone who'd lost someone, even if it was in
a very different sort of way, she couldn't imagine ever
being as careless about it as Mae seemed to be.

"It was a gradual sort of disappearing," Mae said.
"Louise and I didn't see each other every day, you know.
So it wasn't as if she missed a long-standing appointment
one day. We met up when we met up, and by the time I
thought 'Where has that Louise gone?' she might have
already been gone a good long while."

She gave Sophia a smile that wasn't a smile. "Sometimes, that's the way it goes. I don't know what happened to her. Maybe she found a job someplace else.
Maybe she found new love. Or maybe, just maybe, she
really did cross over into another world."

The next bus was headed homeward. Sophia and

DJ thanked Mae for her story and said their good-byes before boarding.

"What do you think?" Sophia whispered as they went up the stairs.

"I think . . ." DJ trailed off. "I don't have any tokens for my stepdad."

Sophia hadn't thought that would be the part of Mae's story that he'd zone in on, but it made sense.

"My stepdad doesn't even exist—at least not here in town."

"But you have your drawings," Sophia said. "You have a ton of them, and they're so detailed. I bet they'd be enough."

DJ shrugged. "Hopefully. It's weird, isn't it? I mean, in that world, this guy came to our town, and met my mom, and they hit it off, and got married and everything. But in this world, he's not even around. I've been looking for years—I used to go sit in the grocery store, or at the mall, and just see if I could find him in the crowd."

"Maybe he lives in the city," Sophia said. There were thousands more people there than in their little town. "Maybe in that other world, he got a job here. Or he decided the city was too crowded."

DJ nodded. "Or a million other things could have happened—a million big things, or a million little things that added up in just the right ways."

They fell quiet, thinking about all the things that could have been, and weren't.

The last passenger boarded the bus. The doors squeaked shut, and the driver pulled from the curb.

"Hey—" DJ half stood. "Mae's trying to tell us something."

The old woman hurried toward the bus, Jimmy running alongside her.

"One second!" Sophia shouted to the driver. He slammed on the brakes. The other people on the bus gave her exasperated looks, but she ignored them. Together, she and DJ shoved at the rusty bus window until it popped open on its hinges.

"What is it?" she shouted to Mae.

"You have to hold it in your mind!" she shouted back. She was completely out of breath. "The world you want to cross into—you have to be able to picture it as clearly as humanly possible. Louise said that. You have to be able to *see* it, to believe in it like you believe in gravity or the moon—"

"Get off the bus if you want to chat," the bus driver called back to them. "We have a schedule to keep."

"You hear me?" Mae said.

"I heard you!" Sophia said.

"Good luck!" Mae said. She disappeared as the bus zoomed around the corner.

22

MAE'S PARTING WORDS ECHOED IN SOPHIA'S thoughts.

You have to be able to see it, to believe in it like you believe in gravity or the moon.

Could Sophia see life with her mother that clearly? She had the Memories, of course, and that made things easier. But they were still just snippets. Were they enough to be Sophia's guide to a whole other world?

Her mother had been a real human being, once upon a time. Since her death, she'd eroded into memories and aching and dust.

Sophia needed better than that.

"You're spending a lot of time on this solar eclipse

project," Sophia's dad said at dinner that night.

"Hmm." Sophia stirred at her chicken and rice, too distracted to say anything else. Today must have been a good day, or at least an okay day, because her dad had finished making dinner by the time she came home, and the TV was on, and he'd scolded her for not giving him a heads-up about staying so long at Luke's.

"How's it going? Learn anything interesting?"

Instead of answering, Sophia blurted out, "Did Mom like living here?"

The silence that followed was like the crest of a wave, the held breath before a thousand tons of water came crashing down.

But there was no crash. Only her dad clearing his throat and saying quietly, "Sometimes she did. Why?"

"I was just wondering." Sophia mushed a piece of chicken into her rice until it was completely buried. "Why sometimes?"

"Why sometimes?" her dad echoed. He stared back at her, and Sophia hated how lost he looked, how unsure. She didn't want to make him feel that way.

"You said she liked living here sometimes." Sophia spoke as quickly as she could, before she lost her courage. "That means sometimes she didn't. Why?"

"Different reasons, I guess." It seemed to take him a lot of effort to get the words out of his mouth. It was as if thinking of Sophia's mother made his tongue stutter, made his jaw go numb. "She got tired of how small the town is. She didn't like how everyone can be in everyone else's business. She dreamed about seeing the rest of the world someday."

"Oh," Sophia said. "Okay."

He cleared his throat. "That all you wanted to know?"

It wasn't. It wasn't even close.

"Did she like chicken and rice?" she asked.

He stared at her in surprise. Then he grinned, and laughed, and kept on laughing. The knot in Sophia's chest loosened, just a touch.

"I don't know if she felt strongly about it one way or another," he said. "Why, what do you think about chicken and rice?"

She made a face. "It's okay if the rice isn't all gloopy."

"No gloopy rice," her dad said. "I'll make a mental note."

Sophia giggled.

"She liked chicken cacciatore," he said. "Chicken

cacciatore with pasta. The spiral kind, not the tube-y ones. She was very specific about her pasta, your mother."

His eyes drifted as he spoke, lingering over the crowded countertops of their tiny kitchen. This was the only home Sophia had ever lived in. The only house her parents had ever lived in together, bequeathed to them after the death of Sophia's grandmother.

When her father looked around like this, Sophia knew he saw her mother. Maybe he didn't have Memories like she did, but the What Might Have Beens had their own way of dragging him under.

By the time his gaze focused back on Sophia, his expression was solemn again.

Sophia pressed her nails into her hand until it hurt. Until she gathered up the courage to say, "I wish I knew more about her."

His face pinched. But Sophia couldn't take the words back now. She didn't want to. They were true. She'd just been too scared these last seven years to say anything about it.

The investigation into the eclipse had changed things. She'd do whatever it took to get her mother back.

Her father took a long, slow breath. "I guess you must. I guess that's natural."

Sophia said nothing, just fidgeted with her fingers.

"All right," her father said. "All right. Let's see. . . ."

He set down his fork. Stared at his rice as if it might tell him something. Cleared his throat again.

"Well," he said quietly, "the most important thing for you to know is that your mother was a—a really lovely person, Sophia. Just a really good person."

Sophia clasped her hands to keep them still. "I know."

Her dad nodded. "Just wanted to make sure. Now, the second most important thing for you to know is that your mother could not sing if her life depended on it."

Sophia was so startled that she burst out laughing.

"I'm serious," her dad said. "Small woodland creatures died when your mother sang. Just keeled right over. That's why she was so thrilled that you could hold a tune."

Sophia flashed back to the Memory of her in the auditorium at school. The way her mom had beamed at her.

She smiled. "What else?"

It took her dad a moment to start speaking again, but he did. He told Sophia about the snacks her mother had

liked to eat when it got past midnight. The music she'd
sing to (badly) on road trips. The places around town
where they used to hang out when they first started
dating, where time seemed to flow slower than it did in
other places, bubbling around them and cocooning them
from the rest of the world.

His voice got quieter and quieter as he spoke. Sophia
coaxed him along for as long as she could, but eventually
it got too hard. Whatever magic she'd tapped into, it was
gone.

Her father busied himself with his dinner, then asked
her if she wanted to go swimming next week.

Sophia let him change the subject.

Her mother had liked chicken cacciatore. Her mother
had wanted to see the world, and had been a terrible
singer, and had eaten probably three tons of salt-and-
vinegar chips during her life.

In the grand scheme of things, that wasn't a whole lot
to know about a person.

But it was a start.

That night, after her father left for his shift at the
law office, Sophia dragged a dining chair under their

attic trapdoor and balanced on it to reach the latch. The trapdoor creaked open like a warning. The stairs unfolded, slowly at first, then tumbling down with a crash.

Sophia held her breath until the dust cleared. Then, ever so slowly, she crept her way up the steps. It had been years since she'd been in the attic. Her dad went up once or twice a year to bring out their winter bedding or Christmas decorations, but otherwise, the space sat untouched.

Here lived the last remnants of her mother's things.

Mae had said they'd need tokens for the crossing, items that would connect them to where they wanted to go. So Sophia needed her mother's possessions.

No matter how weird it felt to be up here.

The attic air felt thicker than the air elsewhere. It sank, hot and heavy, into Sophia's lungs.

The first thing she saw, to her surprise, was her old tricycle. She'd loved it once upon a time—had wanted to ride it every minute of the day. She'd cried when it fell out of her father's truck, one of the wheel rims bent beyond repair. Her parents had kept it by the pantry, promising her they'd buy a new wheel.

But money was tight, and in the meantime, Sophia learned to ride a two-wheeler from the girls down the street. The tricycle sat forgotten until it disappeared. Sophia had assumed her parents had thrown it away or sold it.

Now it sat in front of her, layered in dust.

Her heart pounded for no reason. She walked past the tricycle, toward the cardboard boxes pushed against the wall. The first couple were labeled in her father's handwriting.

Christmas, they said. And *Winter*. The worn flaps parted slightly to reveal piles of plastic ornaments.

The boxes farther back were sealed shut with brown packing tape. If she opened them, her dad would know— even if she resealed the boxes. And being up here, staring at these boxes, wanting to open them, felt like a betrayal somehow. Like something shameful.

She ran her fingers over a strip of tape. She'd brought a paring knife from the kitchen drawer. Just as she pressed the edge of it against the tape, she realized what she'd missed before—the tape she was about to cut wasn't the only layer of tape. There were more layers under it, their edges jagged from being sliced apart.

Her father had opened these boxes before. More than once, judging by the amount of tape they bore.

He'd sealed them, opened them, and sealed them again.

Over and over and over, he'd come up here and looked at the parts of her mother he'd decided Sophia no longer needed to see.

Sophia's anger went into the knife, and the knife plunged into the box. She wrenched it out again a second later, terrified she'd destroyed something.

She cut the rest of the tape more carefully, then lifted the flaps of the box.

Inside: a foam-green cardigan, a photograph, a plastic hairbrush, a clear bag of makeup, a pair of fuzzy pink socks, a slightly misshapen cheerleading statuette.

Sophia hadn't known her mother had been a cheerleader. She sifted through her memory, searching for a hint she'd forgotten. Any mention her mom had ever made about cheerleading. She hadn't been all that far out of high school when Sophia had been born—she should have said *something*, right? If it had been a big part of her life?

But when Sophia dug into the box to free the statuette,

she saw the words JESSUP MIDDLE SCHOOL engraved across the bottom, below the words MOST TENACIOUS.

So her mother had been a cheerleader in middle school. Maybe it hadn't been a big deal. But she'd liked something about the experience enough to keep this old trophy. Why had she cared enough to keep it, but not cared enough to tell Sophia about it?

Maybe she had, but Sophia had forgotten?

Maybe she hadn't, but would have told Sophia someday, if she hadn't died.

Sophia dug deeper into the box. There was a good amount of clothing—a couple of blouses, a pair of worn jeans, a squashed baseball cap, a lacy white summer dress. A collection of gummy, dried-up nail polish clattered around the bottom. Light purple. Midnight blue. A flashing, fish-scale silver. She took those out too, and then the box was empty.

There were two more boxes. Sophia scooped out clothes and jewelry and knickknacks until she sat surrounded by a graveyard of her mother's things.

She rocked back onto her knees. The attic was getting stuffier by the second. And she still needed to choose what she'd take for the solar eclipse.

It would be easier to cart stuff downstairs and look at it there. But just opening these boxes was bad enough. Taking her mother's things downstairs was unthinkable. It would be hours before her dad came home from work, but Sophia couldn't relax until everything was packed away again.

No, she'd have to pick something up here.

She held up the bottles of nail polish, looking at the way they captured the light, imagining her mother holding them.

No, it wasn't personal enough. Neither was the hairbrush, which looked like anything she might have found in the toiletries aisle of the grocery store. She liked the photo, which showed her mother laughing at the camera in cutoff jeans and a loose tank top. In it, she looked barely older than Nicole. But maybe a photograph wasn't a good idea either.

She ended up choosing the cheerleading statuette and the pair of fuzzy socks that had been worn so often the bottoms of them were flat and matted, barely fuzzy at all anymore. Out of all the items in the boxes, they seemed the most unique, and perhaps the most special. Things that had mattered to her mother.

She stacked the rest of her mother's things neatly back where she'd found them.

She got new tape from the kitchen drawer and taped up the boxes and pushed them back into place behind the Christmas decorations.

She crept back down the stairs, silent as a ghost.

23

TWO DAYS BEFORE THE SOLAR ECLIPSE,
Sophia, DJ, and Luke turned in their group project: "Solar
Eclipses and the Destruction of the Established Order."
Mr. Rae lifted an eyebrow at the title and coughed away
what sounded like a laugh before saying, "Great job,
guys. I can't wait to read it."

Sophia gave him a sleepy smile. She and DJ had been
up half the night at Luke's house, piecing together the
final touches on their essay.

And talking about their plans for the eclipse, of
course.

All three of them had chosen their tokens. For
Sophia: the statuette and the socks. For DJ: ten of his

best drawings of his stepfather. For Luke: an old stuffed animal pilfered from the sacred trunk of his sister's things.

Sophia had the statuette and socks with her right now, wrapped in a towel and stuffed in her book bag.

Ostensibly, it was so her dad wouldn't stumble upon them in her room. But mostly, Sophia just liked to have them close, to know that she could hug her book bag against her and feel her mother's things inside.

That night she found herself outside Mr. Scot's front door again. It was early evening. It didn't hit her until she was standing outside the man's house that this was probably a bad idea. The sun was setting—she hadn't expected it to set so soon. And she hadn't parted ways with Mr. Scot on the best of terms last time.

She raised her hand and knocked.

Mr. Scot answered. He looked as he always did: neat, frowning, distant. His frown deepened when his eyes fell on Sophia. He squinted past her into the gathering night.

"It's just me." Sophia's voice felt very small. "Can I come in?"

For a moment, she thought he'd shut the door in her face. Ignore her. She could already feel the preemptive hurt of it, like muscle memory.

"Have you seen Schrödinger?" he asked instead. "He's gone missing again."

She shook her head. "I can help you look for him."

Mr. Scot sighed. "All right," he said, and it sounded like, *If you must.* "Come in."

"Have you thought about getting him a bell?" Sophia asked.

"A bell defeats the purpose of a cat," Mr. Scot said. "It would be embarrassing for him. No, no—keep up. I don't want you wandering off by yourself again."

He shot her an accusatory look, which Sophia pretended not to see. Together, they scoured the living room for signs of Schrödinger. Sophia knelt to check underneath the couch, while Mr. Scot shone a penlight behind some wooden shelves.

There was no cat to be found. She stood—and nearly jumped out of her skin when Mr. Scot cried out.

The heavy oak shelves collapsed a second later. Their contents hailed down—books and pens and a jar of dead flowers. Sophia screamed, covering her head with her arms. Something struck her on her shoulder. She fell, hard.

"Sophia?" Mr. Scot shouted as the dust began to settle. "Sophia! Are you all right?"

Sophia was too disorientated to reply. Her fingers closed around the thing that had hit her—a small glass bowl.

"Sophia!" Mr. Scot called again.

"I'm—I'm all right," she said. It seemed to be true. Her shoulder ached, but she climbed easily to her feet. "Are you—"

She cut off as she caught sight of Mr. Scot. He lay trapped beneath the shelving, pinned like a bug to the ground.

"If you'd give me a hand," he said, out of breath. Sophia shoved at the fallen bookcase until Mr. Scot wriggled out. They were both out of breath by the end of the ordeal. Sophia plopped down beside Mr. Scot on the ground. He nursed his left arm—the same arm she'd seen bandaged a few days ago.

"Thank you," he said. He noticed her rubbing at her shoulder. "Are you all right?"

Sophia nodded. "I got hit by that bowl over there."

She reached over to pick it up. It was a delicate, colorful thing—sunshine yellow at the rim before melting seamlessly into orange, and then a deep red as it reached its base. Little bubbles sat frozen in the glass.

Beside it lay a small piece of amber half-wrapped in linen, and a tube of lipstick.

"Ah," said Mr. Scot sadly. He scooped the amber and lipstick into the bowl, then cradled everything in his lap. For a long moment, he just stared at it and seemed to forget all else.

Sophia looked at the jumbled mess of shelving behind them. It would take all night to clean up. And even then, she wasn't sure whether the shelves were salvageable.

"Did you fall?" She couldn't imagine how else such a large, heavy thing would have tilted over by itself.

Her question shook Mr. Scot from his reverie. "Yes, yes, something like that," he said.

Sophia had more questions, but she was interrupted by a black-and-white blur streaking into the room. Schrödinger lapped twice around Sophia's feet before plopping down in front of Mr. Scot, meowing piteously as if Mr. Scot had been lost, and not the other way around.

"Where have you been?" scolded Mr. Scot. "Did you go to Luke's house again?"

Resin, Sophia thought suddenly. The golden lump wrapped in linen hadn't been amber, but the resin used for stringed instruments. She'd seen pieces of it in the orchestra room at school.

"We're going to try to cross," she said. "The day after tomorrow, during the eclipse."

Mr. Scot stilled. He looked at her, studying the line of her mouth, the set of her eyes, then turned to Schrödinger. "And how are you going to do that?"

"We heard a story," Sophia said. "I came to tell you about it, in case you wanted to know. In case you wanted to try too."

He'd never admitted to her that this was what he wished to do, but he didn't need to. The pieces fit. Besides, Sophia recognized in Mr. Scot the same quiet longing that dwelled in herself. In DJ. In Luke.

Mr. Scot didn't reply. Stayed silent even as Sophia told him about Mae's story. About the tokens. About the need to picture as clearly as he could the world where he wished to go.

She petted Schrödinger as she spoke, so she didn't have to look Mr. Scot in the eye. It was easier that way.

"So what about you?" he asked, once she finished speaking. "You have all the things you need for this . . . crossing?"

It was hard to say. Sophia had her mother's statuette and socks, and the things her father had told her. Would that be enough?

She shrugged and sank her fingers into Schrödinger's fur. "I'm not even sure it'll actually work."

"There are no guarantees," Mr. Scot agreed.

She forced herself to face him. "What do you think? Don't talk in circles. Just tell me. I know you've been looking into eclipses for a long time. I know you've been poking around Donway Shallows, and that you know all these things about parallel universes. I know you said that you've never heard of people crossing worlds before, but—do you think this could be a way? Do *you* think it'll work?"

There was something unreadable in his eyes. Something like sadness, but more complicated. "I think you shouldn't be disappointed, all right?"

Sophia was used to disappointment. If need be, she would bear it, as she always had.

"Don't be disappointed," Mr. Scot repeated softly. "Either way."

24

THE NIGHT BEFORE THE SOLAR ECLIPSE,
Sophia and her dad stood at the sink, washing dishes.
Her dad had been in a good mood today. She felt a rush
of affection for him as he hummed off-key and pushed
his hair from his face with sudsy hands.

"Guess I'm overdue for a haircut, huh?" he said when
he caught her looking.

"Want me to do it?" Sophia asked. He'd let her trim
the back of his head, the parts he couldn't reach himself,
since she was eight years old.

"Sure. Let's do it tomorrow after school."

Sophia nodded before remembering that tomorrow
after school was post–solar eclipse. Would she still be

here to cut her father's hair? Would another version of Sophia be here instead?

Or would she simply leave a blankness behind, as if she'd never existed?

It was a frightening thought. She couldn't leave her father alone—he needed her.

But if she crossed, she'd just enter another world, with another version of her father. So she wouldn't *really* be leaving him, would she?

Her dad interrupted her thoughts. "Remember how you asked if Mom liked living here, and I said that sometimes she didn't? Sometimes she got tired of how small things are, how everyone gets in everyone else's business?"

"Yeah?" Sophia said cautiously. They hadn't spoken about her mother since that night, and it wasn't like him to bring it up again all by himself. It was unfamiliar ground, and she stepped carefully.

"How about you? You ever feel like that?"

Sophia shrugged and rinsed off another plate. "I guess."

"So what do you think? Should we move?"

"Should we *what*?" Sophia stared at her dad, her eyes

wide, her wet hands dripping onto her shirt. "You want to move? Why?"

"Why not?" He was smiling, and it was almost a real smile. "Don't you think it would be cool? We could go anywhere we wanted."

"What about Tom's? And your job in the city?"

He shrugged. The plates in the sink lay forgotten, slowly drowning in suds. "Tom would find someone else. And I'd find other jobs. You could go to another school."

Sophia wasn't sure things worked like that. She remembered when her dad used to work at a hardware store a few years ago, until they'd closed down. She remembered how long it had been until he'd found his current job downtown.

And definitely, it wasn't as simple as *You could go to another school.*

Once upon a time, Sophia might not have minded the idea. She knew every kid who went to their school— had known them, and their siblings, and their families for as long as she remembered. Which meant they'd known her, too. Other than the odd fight or reconciliation, everyone already knew who their friends were, and they weren't looking for new ones.

And somewhere, somehow, Sophia had found herself fallen between the cracks. A forgotten thing.

But now she had DJ. She even had Luke, in a weird sort of way.

"That's not fair." She clenched her fists. "You've never—you've never even talked about moving before."

Her dad looked at her in surprise. "Sophia, it's just a thought. Nothing's decided. I wouldn't make any decisions without talking about it with you first."

"You would," she protested. "We never talk about anything! Whenever anything bad happens, you just go to bed and pull the blinds and lie there, and you don't tell me what's *wrong.*"

She was being hurtful now, cutting where she knew he was already wounded, and she was almost too upset to care.

Her dad returned to washing the dishes. His face had gone rigid, his body angled away from her. "You don't have to worry about things like that."

As if it were that easy.

Sophia stood there as long as she could stand it, listening to the sound of the dishes clinking in the sink, the quiet splash of the water, the hum of the refrigerator. The unsaid words that sank ever heavier into her stomach.

I do, she wanted to say.

I worry.

I worry all the time.

But what was the point?

She walked out of the kitchen. Kept going until she was up the stairs, was in her bedroom. She curled up underneath the covers and turned her back to the door.

She listened to see if her father would follow her, but he didn't. The floorboards creaked, and Sophia heard the telltale sounds of her father pacing through the house. Soon he'd need to leave for work.

The stairs groaned. She held her breath.

Her father came to the door and opened it. Sophia closed her eyes, trying to pretend that what had happened in the kitchen hadn't upset her, that she'd come up here and fallen asleep as if nothing were wrong.

He didn't come. She opened her eyes again.

She ached to turn and see what he was doing. But she was stubborn, and she was proud, and she stayed facing the wall, her eyes open, her body still.

Her father closed the door.

A while later, she heard the front door open and

shut. The sound of the truck as it backed into the road.

It doesn't matter, she told herself as she curled up tighter. Tomorrow was the solar eclipse. Tomorrow things would work out the way they rarely did for her.

She would go to the abandoned mill. She would take her mother's things.

She would wait for the eclipse.

And once it came, once she crossed into that world where her mother had never left her, everything would be all right.

But she couldn't stop thinking about the way her dad had stiffened as she yelled at him. The way he'd turned away from her, as if Sophia were something he needed to shield himself against.

She flipped over and over in bed, thinking about all the better ways she could have acted, all the better ways other Sophias in other universes would have acted, until she finally fell asleep.

25

SOPHIA WOKE WITH A LURCH, HER HEART fluttering in her chest, the rest of her body excited before her brain could remember why.

When she remembered, her heart pounded even harder. Today was the day.

Today was the day.

At 10:05 today, the sun would go black, and the town would fall dark.

Then maybe, just maybe, Sophia's whole world would change forever.

She padded downstairs and ventured into the silent kitchen, half hoping that her dad had stayed late again. When it became obvious that he hadn't, she searched for a note. When she found none, she reminded herself that it didn't matter.

In a universe where her mother had never died, Sophia and her dad would never have had that fight. Sophia would never have run up to her bed.

She just had to wait for the eclipse.

She couldn't even think about breakfast. She stuffed her things into her book bag and sleepwalked to school, muddled her way indoors, and sat trembling in her seat through homeroom. Through first period. Through second period.

Her teachers talked but made no sense. Her fellow students laughed and whispered and shouted to one another in the halls, but they were just blurs of color.

Sophia patted the cheerleading-statuette-shaped lump in her hoodie pocket and wished the weather were cooler. She looked out of place wearing so much, and she'd been sweating all morning.

To calm herself, she went over the plan she'd made with DJ and Luke. When everyone filed outdoors for the solar eclipse, they'd wait for their teachers to do a head count, then slip away and meet by the maple tree at the edge of the soccer field.

Then together they'd head for the woods.

She was moving in a daze toward her third-period classroom when she ran into DJ. He pulled her to the edge of the hall and whispered, "Luke's suspended."

His words blasted the clouds from Sophia's mind. "*What?*"

"He got in a fight with an administrator," DJ said. "I think he threw something at her. I don't know. He's suspended for two days. He isn't here."

Sophia propelled DJ through the hall until they found a more private alcove "But he can still make it to the mill, right?"

DJ shook his head. His hand was in his pocket, where Sophia assumed he was hiding his cell phone. "He's stuck at home with a babysitter. There's no way he's getting out the door without her noticing."

Sophia groaned, digging the heels of her hands into her temples. Why couldn't Luke just rein things in? Why couldn't he keep it together?

DJ checked his phone. He hesitated, then added, "He says we should go without him."

Sophia shook her head. "We can't do that. It wouldn't be fair."

"Well, if he's stuck at home—"

"Then we'll go get him," Sophia said.

The warning bell rang for third period. She squeezed DJ's wrist. "We meet at the maple tree like we planned. We'll figure it out."

Her third-period teacher, Ms. Brandt, gave up all pretense of holding class and just called on kids to talk about cool astrological events they'd experienced. Sophia half listened to muddled accounts of harvest moons and glimpses of Venus, before they were interrupted by the announcement directing seventh-grade classes to gather outside.

She bumped her hip against the edge of her desk as she stood. Nearly tipped her chair over when she tried to slide it in.

She had a flash of her mother's face as she fumbled through the doors—so sharp it was almost like a Memory. It was gone by the time she stepped outside, replaced by a growing sense of urgency.

The day was still bright, not a single cloud in the blue sky. No hint at all that in twenty minutes, the world would fall dark.

DJ hovered at the edge of his class. As Sophia watched, he cast one last glance at his teacher, then slipped into the class next to his—then the one even farther away—before breaking off entirely and blending into the trees.

Sophia stayed stuck where she was, waiting stupidly for Ms. Brandt to find "Menkle, Denis"—who never, ever made it to the same place as the rest of the class.

She scuffed her already too-scuffed sneakers against the blacktop and scowled as Denis Menkle was called for again and again until he was finally found, lost and uncaring, by the sixth-grade classes. An eon later, Ms. Brandt got to the Ws, and finally, to Sophia.

"Here!" Sophia shouted, louder than necessary. She waited five more minutes after that, just to be safe.

She didn't bother leaving in stages. She just moved purposefully, and no one said a word, not even when she broke through the edge of the last class.

DJ waited for her at the maple tree. Maybe it was only Sophia's imagination, but the air around them seemed a little strange—a little *different* than it had been before, when they'd first come outside.

"We've only got fifteen minutes," he told her urgently.

He didn't say *We might miss it if we go get Luke*, but Sophia knew what he was thinking. She was thinking it too.

Still.

They couldn't go without Luke. Luke, who was ornery, and utterly lacking in manners, and didn't know when to keep his mouth shut. Luke, who missed his sister, and felt so trapped in this life without her—this life where she was gone, and he was the one left behind.

Luke wasn't always Sophia's favorite person, but she understood him now. At least, better than she had before.

He, DJ, Sophia—they were in this together.

"Come on," she said, and they ran.

Luck blessed them at the bus stop; the bus arrived just seconds after they did. They rushed aboard, throwing themselves into a seat and tapping their feet anxiously as the driver waited a minute or two more before setting off again. Sophia pressed her forehead against the window and counted the minutes until they pulled up to the stop nearest Luke's house.

Then she and DJ were off again, sprinting down the sidewalk. They skidded to a stop outside Luke's house. Logically, Sophia knew it looked no different from the other times she'd seen it—eggshell white, two-storied, with a small front porch and black roof. But it had never seemed as fortresslike as it did now.

A beat-up old car sat in the driveway, the rear bumper decorated with stickers. Luke's babysitter?

DJ had been texting madly on the bus, and he gestured for Sophia to follow him around back. They snuck into the yard. Luke was already pushing his bedroom window open, pressing his face against the bug screen.

The sunlight was definitely dimmer now, the shadows of Luke's face stark and deep. Sophia trembled with something half excitement, half fear.

"You guys are crazy," Luke hissed. "It's already started. You're going to miss totality."

"Just come downstairs," Sophia shouted.

"*Shhh,*" Luke said. "She'll hear you. And I can't. *She's* downstairs."

"Can you take the screen off?" Sophia said.

He did as she suggested, fiddling with the window screen until it came away in his hands. He leaned out. "Now what?"

"I don't know," Sophia said. "Tie your sheets together or something."

"I don't think I have any sheets," Luke snapped. He

looked behind him, was about to go check, when DJ said, "Just jump, Luke—we'll catch you."

Sophia wasn't sure about this plan, but they were running out of time. Luke wavered a moment, then nodded. He tossed his book bag down first. Then he climbed out onto the window ledge and swung his legs over.

"Don't drop me," he warned.

He twisted around, lowering himself as far as he could until he was dangling from his fingertips. Then he let go.

Sophia and DJ braced themselves, but it didn't help. They hit the ground in a heap. Someone, Sophia wasn't sure who, let out a strangled yelp.

"Luke?" a girl called from within the house.

Luke jumped up—grabbed DJ and Sophia's arms to help them up too. *"Hurry, hurry,"* he hissed.

"Luke? Was that you?"

Sophia's ankle felt funny, but she hobbled to her feet and ignored it. Luke led the way, directing them through a gap in the shrubbery and out onto the sidewalk.

They darted down the street while his babysitter shouted after them.

*   *   *

The woods around Donway Shallows were even colder than they'd been before. Sophia was glad for her sweatshirt. The boys shivered as they stepped into the gutted building. Around them, the woods stood bathed in a strange, unnatural twilight.

Without discussion, they converged at the coldest spot. Sophia took out her mother's statuette and fuzzy socks. She glanced at DJ, who stood with his sketches cradled against his chest, and at Luke, who clutched his sister's stuffed dog.

"Should we, I don't know, hold hands or something?" she blurted. She figured that if she didn't say it, no one would.

"Why?" Luke said.

DJ said, "We might not end up going to the same place, right?"

That was true. If there were a billion billion parallel universes, who was to say that the same one would take all three of them?

Sophia had already known that.

But it had never hit her as hard as it did now, standing here in the cold, growing dark, watching her friends— her first, *real, good* friends—as their faces went dim.

No matter what, any universe she ended up in should have a Luke and a DJ, right? But would they still be friends? In a universe where Sophia's mother had never died, would she still care?

I would, Sophia thought. *I would. I would.*

There wasn't time to think about it more. She closed her eyes and conjured up a picture of her mother. Remembered her so fiercely that it hurt like a too-hard hug.

Someone reached out and grabbed her hand. Her eyes flew open, but she saw nothing. Just blackness.

The hand around hers disappeared, dissolved away like a dream.

26

SHE WAS ALONE.

No DJ. No Luke.

She called their names. Got nothing back but the echo of her voice. The sun shone as if it had never gone away. Sophia wrapped her arms around herself. For a long, long moment, she didn't move from her spot. Not even an inch.

Had it worked?

She shouted again, and her voice wavered. Had the boys left her? Had they disappeared?

She squeezed her arms. Told herself to snap out of it. She needed to take stock of things.

She was alone.

She was still at Donway Shallows, which looked just as she remembered it, abandoned and crumbling.

She no longer wore her sweatshirt. In fact, she was in a completely different set of clothing, a perky sky-blue dress that wasn't at all her style. Her hair was up. She patted awkwardly at the curled ends.

Was it still Friday? Was it still a school day?

Maybe she'd find DJ and Luke back at Jessup. She felt better with a goal in mind. She'd head to school first, get a better handle on things. Figure out the ins and outs of what had just occurred.

Then and only then would she let herself think about home.

Jessup reverberated with the shouting and thundering feet of the school hallway in between classes. Visitors were only supposed to come in through the front door and check in at the office, but Sophia had discovered an unlocked side door at the start of the year.

Lots of kids knew about it, as did some of the teachers. But a broken lock was low on the list of things that needed fixing at Jessup, and kids often took advantage of it to sneak into school late.

Everything at Jessup seemed to be the same. Same hallway. Same kids. Same—

DJ.

He lingered at the far end of the hall, tying his shoes. He looked like he always did—artsy, bookish, too smart by half for Jessup and the other kids.

"DJ!" Sophia shouted.

Their eyes met. He was in his usual DJ uniform of collared shirt and dark shorts and purple sneakers, his book bag slung over one shoulder. He gave her a confused quirk of his eyebrows as he stood. It startled Sophia so much that she could only stare blankly back, even as DJ gave her a polite nod before going on his way.

He didn't know her.

At least, he didn't know her as more than just another face in his class. Another girl he'd attended school with for years but never bothered getting to know.

Sophia stayed rooted to the middle of the hall. Now that she was paying closer attention, she did notice other things that were off: the COUNTDOWN TO SUMMER display was missing; the teachers' names on the doors were all switched around; she was pretty sure she didn't recognize some of the kids streaming past her—

"Sophia?" a girl said, yanking her from her daze.

Lacey Wilkens. She smiled at Sophia, her dimples flashing. "Where are you going? Social studies is that way."

"R-Right," Sophia stuttered.

Lacey looped her arm with Sophia's like they were best friends and launched into gossip about the end-of-year dance and some boy who'd never been in their class back in—well, back in the other universe. The one Sophia had come from.

What else had changed? Since when did Lacey—bubbly, pretty, wickedly funny—chat with Sophia in the halls? She was struck by a powerful relief that she was still at the right school, in the right town. That the world hadn't tipped too far on its axis.

Lacey dragged her to their social studies classroom. Sophia only caught a glimpse of the nameplate before Lacey pulled her inside: MS. KENT.

They hadn't had a Ms. Kent before. Ms. Kent, who was small, and old, and—

Sophia gasped.

Mae stood at the head of the classroom like it was her kingdom. Sophia recognized the half scowl on her face, the vivid gleam in her blue eyes. She was less familiar with the fashionable dress Mae wore, or the neat bun she'd pinned against the back of her head.

"Something wrong?" she said, arching an eyebrow at Sophia.

Sophia stuttered a few nonsense words before Lacey yanked her to her desk.

The Mae of this world was a social studies teacher. *Sophia's* social studies teacher. She bit back a gleeful laugh. What a strange but wonderful thing.

She couldn't stop staring at Mae—at Ms. Kent. Did she still have a terrier named Jimmy? It was hard to imagine this woman as the same woman who'd lived beneath the sheet metal at Donway Shallows.

Lacey was still talking. "So anyway, he gets all stupidly worked up, the way he always does, and he goes *crazy* on the janitor's trash can. One of those big ones, you know? He starts punching and kicking at it like it killed his dog or something. I think he's going to get suspended—"

"Wait," Sophia said, perking up. "Who? Luke?"

Maybe circumstances had made it so that she and DJ had never become friends, but that didn't mean the same had happened between her and Luke.

She ached for someone familiar. Someone who'd act the way she expected them to act.

Even Luke's scowl would be brilliant.

Lacey frowned. "Who?"

"Luke. Luke McPherson?"

Lacey stared at Sophia in confusion.

"What?" Sophia tried not to stiffen under the scrutiny of Lacey's eyes.

"Luke McPherson," Lacey said, sounding incredulous. "Are you feeling okay?"

Sophia didn't know how to respond. Lacey dramatically pressed her palm to Sophia's forehead, as if checking for a fever.

Finding none, she leaned closer, her eyes very wide, and said, "Don't you remember that Luke McPherson's dead?"

Ten minutes into Ms. Kent's class, Sophia raised her hand and asked to go to the nurse's office. She didn't care that her question made everyone turn and stare at her, hoping she might do something exciting like throw up or faint.

She did neither. Just said, quietly, "I don't feel good."

"All right," Ms. Kent said, and didn't argue when Sophia packed up her things.

"You okay?" Lacey whispered as Sophia passed her desk. There was real concern on her face, and however unaccustomed Sophia was to having Lacey as a friend, she felt a surge of gratitude.

Friends, she knew, could be hard to come by.

"I'm okay," she assured Lacey, and gave her a lopsided smile before slipping from the room.

When she'd raised her hand, she really had meant to go to the nurse's office. But now, standing alone in the hall, it seemed like a meaningless destination. The nurse would take her temperature and tell her to lie down. Sophia didn't have a fever.

She just needed to get home.

She set off before she had time to change her mind. The school's side door wasn't far from the nurse's office anyhow. It was all too easy to run off.

The empty back lot gave her the chills. The last time she'd seen it, it had been filled with kids and teachers. Now it lay starkly empty.

The path back home was more or less unchanged. Maybe a few of her neighbors had different-looking lawns, but that could also just be her imagination.

The car in her driveway was definitely new. At least to Sophia. It was smallish and dark blue, the front bumper dented.

A few feet from the front door, she was struck by a thought: What if she no longer lived here? What if none of this was hers?

But no, her key still fit in the lock, and the knob turned just fine, and she took one, two, three baby steps into the hall.

Mom, she thought.

But when she opened her mouth, what came out instead, driven by habit and fear, was: "Dad?"

Her voice echoed a little. *There's no one here,* she thought.

She almost went right back out the door again, just to take a minute to catch her breath. To ready herself for the rest of the house.

But as she turned to go, she heard a faint *thump* from the far end of the house.

She froze. Half of her urged her to call out again. The other half stifled her into silence.

That half won. She padded cautiously toward the source of the noise. It came from the kitchen.

She sidled up against the wall at the end of the hall-way, breath held, gearing up her courage—then peeked around the corner.

The kitchen was empty. A pair of blue-cushioned bar stools stood next to the counter, where no bar stools had ever stood before, but that was the only change Sophia could see.

Other than the attic steps, which had been pulled down.

From this angle, she saw only the bottom of the steps. But as she watched, they began to tremble. She heard the creaking noise of someone descending from above.

The shoes came into view first: soft, yellow flats the color of daisy cores. Then a pair of ankles, and knees, and—

"Oh my *goodness*, Sophie," her mother said, nearly falling in surprise. "You scared the daylights out of me. What are you doing home?"

27

SOPHIA THOUGHT SHE MIGHT THROW UP.

It wasn't the response she'd expected. Here was her mother—now all the way down the attic steps—wearing yellow shoes and khaki shorts and a white tank top, her dark hair falling around her shoulders—and Sophia felt like throwing up. The hallway tipped up on one end.

Her mother cried out, and then Sophia must have tipped over a little herself because the next thing she knew, she was halfway to the floor, and her mom had caught her.

"I don't feel good," Sophia said.

"You're a little warm." Her mom pressed one cool hand against Sophia's forehead, her brow furrowed. "Did you go to the nurse? Why didn't they call me?"

Sophia stared up at her mother's face. It was the same and yet different from the one she remembered. The one she'd seen in photographs. The ones she'd seen in her Memories. Had she always had that cluster of freckles by her hairline? That tiny scar at the edge of her jaw?

"Let's get you to the couch," her mom said, and slung Sophia's arm around her shoulders.

The living room was the living room from Sophia's Memory. The one with the blue couches, and the funny-looking clock, and knickknacks. Now that Sophia had more time, she recognized them as carved horses.

"Did you eat something funny?" her mom was saying—what a strange thing—*her mom was saying*.

Her mom was sitting.

Her mom was stroking her hair.

Her mom was here. Real.

Alive.

"You were fine this morning, weren't you, Sophie?"

Sophie? It was weird, being called *Sophie*.

"I guess," Sophia said, because honestly, she had no idea how *Sophie*—how the Sophia of this universe—had felt this morning.

She tried not to think about it too hard. It made the want-to-throw-up feeling worse. She focused on the warmth of her mother's arm around her. The brush of her mother's fingers through her hair.

She wrapped her arms around her mother's neck and hugged her as hard as she could.

Nothing else matters, she told herself.

And in that moment, she believed it.

Sophia's mom insisted that she stay on the couch for the next half hour, and that she drink some orange juice. Sophia didn't protest. It felt too nice to lie there with her legs on her mother's lap, opening her eyes from time to time to see her flip a page in her book or smile down at Sophia.

"Feel any better?" she asked after a bit, and Sophia nodded sleepily.

The next thing she knew, she was waking from an impromptu nap. The sun had shifted so it streamed in low through the living room windows. Her mother had disappeared from the couch, but Sophia heard her in the kitchen, talking on the phone to someone—a boss, maybe, because she was saying how she needed someone to take her shift today, that Sophia wasn't feeling well.

She returned to the living room a moment later and smiled when she saw Sophia awake.

Back home—it was hard not to think of that universe as *home*—her dad would have been back by now. Maybe things were different here. That made sense.

But when her mom started warming things up for dinner and only put out two place settings at the table, Sophia's stomach tweaked. "Do you think Dad'll get back soon?"

It was like she'd pressed pause on everything.

Her mom stilled, her arm and hand hovering over the table. "What do you mean?"

Sophia didn't like the look on her mother's face. The tightness of her mouth. The controlled blandness around her eyes.

"When is he going to get home?" she said. "From work?"

Her mom sat heavily in her chair.

"You miss him a lot, don't you, Sophie?" she said, and suddenly Sophia couldn't breathe anymore, her throat squeezing up, her lungs collapsing.

Had she made a trade?

Had she exchanged one parent for the other?

"Oh, honey," her mom said, looking distraught. She reached out for Sophia. "Don't do this, Sophie, honey. It'll be all right. You'll see him this weekend."

"This weekend?" Sophia choked out.

"That's right." Now her mom looked confused. "We talked about this, remember?"

Had they?

Why would Sophia only get to see him on the weekends?

Why wouldn't he be here?

Why wouldn't they all be together?

"Come on, honey," her mom said, pasting on a smile. "Let's have dinner, okay? You'll feel better after you've eaten."

But Sophia wasn't sure that would help at all.

28

LITTLE BY LITTLE, SOPHIA COLLECTED
the differences between this world and the one she'd left.

First off, it wasn't Friday here, but Wednesday. Sophia was having a tough time wrapping her head around that one.

The house was the same. Kind of. Her bedroom was still her bedroom. Her sock drawer was still her sock drawer. The bed sat in its usual place in the far right corner. The blankets were different, but the laundry hamper in her closet was right where she'd left it, half-filled with clothing she mostly recognized.

The master bedroom was the most different. In her old universe, her father had kept the room simple, the walls bare. Here, photographs hung at all heights, sat in clusters on the vanity (which didn't exist back in her world) and the dresser (which did).

Sophia held her breath as she looked through them. For most of her life, she'd had extra memories that didn't fit. Now she was missing memories instead. When had she gone to New York City? When had she gone canoeing?

These things had happened—at least in this world. Here was photographic proof of it: Sophia in front of the Empire State Building; Sophia making a face at a canoe paddle dripping wet moss; Sophia with her mom; Sophia with her dad; Sophia with both of them.

And everywhere, happy pictures of her parents together. How could they have gone from that to now?

It had taken slow, careful questioning of her mother over dinner, and a lot of piecing together things unsaid, but Sophia thought she'd figured out the broad strokes of her family's situation.

The crux of it was this: her father had moved out a little less than a month ago. Things hadn't been great between him and Sophia's mother for a long while before that—years, perhaps.

I don't get it, Sophia thought as she got ready for bed.

Back in her own world, it had seemed so obvious where things had gone wrong in her father's life—her mother's death.

If her mother hadn't died, then there would have been no black period of mourning. No gash in the fabric of their family.

No waking up at night and listening to her father cry in the living room, audible even through the buzz of late-night TV.

If her mother had never died, then her family would have had no reason to fall apart.

Except apparently, it still had. For one reason, or a dozen reasons, or a hundred.

A memory came to her—a real memory: Mr. Scot giving her a long, hard look as they sat in his living room. *Don't be disappointed,* he'd said. At the time, Sophia had been sure he'd meant, *Don't be disappointed if things don't work. If the solar eclipse comes and goes and you don't make the crossing.*

What if he'd meant something entirely different?

"Mom?" she called out as she switched off the bedside light. Her mother came in, smiling. Sophia waited until she'd perched on the edge of the bed. Then she said, softly, "You know Luke McPherson? Do you remember him, I mean?"

"Of course," her mom said. "Why're you thinking about him now?"

Sophia shrugged. "Someone brought him up at school today."

"It was all very sad, wasn't it?" She scrunched down and nestled her head against Sophia's shoulder. "I can't imagine, losing two kids like that. All in one night."

Sophia swallowed hard. Had Luke died in the same car accident that had killed his sister? Was that another twist this world was throwing at her?

She pressed against her mother and closed her eyes. She just needed to take this one step at a time. It wasn't as if she'd *caused* any of this to happen, right?

These were just things that had already happened— were already happening alongside all the things happening in Sophia's old universe. All she'd done was drift from one world to another, like a moth between billowing sheets.

In the end, she'd gotten what she wanted. She'd gotten her mother.

Everything else, she could get used to.

Couldn't she?

"You feeling better now?" her mom asked, pressing her lips against Sophia's forehead. Sophia nodded. "You scared me when you came home, you know. The school called. They said you never made it to the nurse's office—you just ran right out of Ms. Kent's class with your things."

Sophia didn't meet her mother's eyes. Of course the school would have called as soon as they figured out she was missing. She was surprised her mother hadn't brought it up earlier.

"Sorry," she said, and pressed even harder against her mother's side. "I just wanted to come home."

Her mom squeezed her shoulder. "You want to get up early with me tomorrow? Make some pancakes together before I leave for the lunch shift?"

"What about school?"

Her mom's nose scrunched up. "Just *how* much better are you feeling?"

Sophia grinned. "Only a little bit, I guess."

"Only a little bit?"

"A very little bit."

"Good. Because we still have those blueberries in the freezer, and I just bought walnuts."

Blueberries and walnuts. Some things, it seemed, just didn't change.

"I love you, Mom," Sophie whispered.

The words had been fluttering inside her stomach all night, hesitant but growing stronger with each passing moment. She felt a great relief once they hit the air—but also a sudden, gut-twisting fear.

A fear that dissipated, dissolved into warm summer air, as her mother said, "Love you, too, Sophie."

As simple, as easy, as if she said it every day.

29

SOPHIA DIDN'T HAVE ANY MEMORIES—
real or otherworldly—of making pancakes with her mother.
Thursday morning was a rush of newness: her mother hum-
ming as she turned on the stove, flicking her wrist as she
folded the pancake batter, laughing when Sophia got flour
on her nose.

It was longer than any Memory, more concrete than
any dream.

It's real, Sophia kept telling herself. *It's real. She's real.*

They sat at the dining table, eating blueberry-and-
walnut pancakes smothered in butter. Her mother
giggled. "What, Sophie?"

"What *what?*" Sophia replied automatically. There

was a huge grin on her face, and she knew it.

"You look like it's Christmas." Her mother waggled her eyebrows. "Or like you've got the world's best secret."

Sophia buried her smile in another bite of pancakes.

She couldn't savor the moment, though. Her mother had to be at work in time for the lunch rush. Before long, she was digging for her keys and slipping on her shoes as Sophia ran the dirty bowls and plates under the faucet.

"See you later, honey." She planted a kiss on Sophia's temple before rushing for the door. "Don't get too wild at home—remember, you're supposed to be sick!"

Then she was gone, and the house was quiet.

Sophia dried the dishes and put them away. She ran her fingers over the smooth, faux-leather couches, trying her hardest to remember all the days and nights Sophia-of-this-world must have sat on them. Then she headed to the master bedroom to study the photos on the dresser—she couldn't get enough of those photos. It was a slide show of a life she'd never lived.

When the phone rang, she answered automatically, expecting a telemarketer. Her brain stuttered when a familiar voice came over the line instead.

"Hello? Maria?"

"Dad?"

"Sophia." He sounded surprised. "What're you doing home?"

"I'm sick," she said automatically, then regretted it when he immediately said, concerned, "Sick? Are you okay?"

"Yeah—it's just a cold."

"Do you want me to come over? Bring you anything?"

"I—"

She hesitated. She did want to see him—she *really* wanted to see him. But things were so muddled in this world. Was she supposed to wait until the weekend, the way her mother had said? Would her mother be upset if her dad came? Would they be breaking some sort of rule?

Would her dad be the same person she knew?

The questions crowded her brain—delayed her reply.

Her father cleared his throat. "It's all right. I'm sure your mother's got it handled. Did she already leave for work?"

"Yeah," Sophia said.

"But you'll let me know if you need anything?"

"Yeah," Sophia said again, lamely.

"I miss you," he said quietly. He didn't seem surprised

by the fumbling, hesitant nature of Sophia's responses. He sounded tired. As tired as he'd sounded those nights back in her old universe, when he was missing her mother the worst. "You know that, right? I'm really looking forward to Saturday."

"Yeah," Sophia whispered. Her chest hurt. "Me too."

There was more after that—chitchat about school and friends that Sophia struggled to get through, because he kept referencing teachers that she had never had, and parties she'd never attended. The Sophia Wallace of this universe was apparently the sort of girl who got invited to parties.

By the time they said good-bye and hung up, Sophia was dizzy with the things she didn't know about herself. She plopped down on the living room sofa and tried to get things straight in her head. But it seemed impossible. There were so many little details. So many shades of difference between the Sophia she'd spent a lifetime becoming and the Sophia she now needed to be.

She wished, fervently, that she could talk things out with DJ.

Except they weren't friends anymore. She had new friends—but she couldn't imagine talking to Lacey about any of this. Did she trust Lacey? Had Other Sophia trusted Lacey?

Other Sophia. What had happened to the Sophia who'd been here before?

Had they traded places, so *that* Sophia was back in the universe where their mother had died?

If she *were* back in Sophia's old universe, was she just as confused as Sophia was now? Did she know how to act? How to take care of their dad when he needed it?

Maybe she didn't. After all, unlike Sophia herself, maybe Other Sophia had never had the chance to learn.

Those thoughts only made her head hurt.

She moved about the house, trying to distract herself with the television, or books, or even just tidying up her room, cataloging all the differences between it and the one she remembered. After a while, she even wished she'd gone to school. At least that would have given her something to do.

The hours dragged until lunch. Then through the afternoon. If Sophia were back in her old world, she might be hanging out with DJ right now.

She pressed the heels of her hands into her temples. She had to stop doing that—thinking about the things she no longer had. She'd come because she wanted her mother to be here, to be alive. And she'd gotten what she wanted.

It wasn't fair of her to want all the good things from her old world too.

Was it?

She didn't know what was right and what was wrong.

Then it struck her. The one remaining person who might understand what she was going through.

The Sophia Wallace of this world had a very nice bike.

Sophia thought it was very nice, anyway. It had shiny handles and a padded seat, and the gears shifted smoothly as she zoomed down the road toward Mr. Scot's home.

Before long, she was huffing and sweating. She cut off the main street and into the shaded back roads. The paths here were dirt instead of concrete, but at least they didn't radiate heat.

What would the Mr. Scot of this world be like? she wondered. Would he still have the same glasses? Would his house still be a mess? Would he still own Schrödinger?

She pumped her legs hard up the next hill, grinning as she reached the crest. A blessedly long stretch of down-sloping path awaited her, passing over a moss-green footbridge before swerving back toward the main street. She let her bike zoom down, gathering speed.

The wind whipped at her hair. She let out a whoop of delight—a whoop that turned into a scream as the footbridge collapsed beneath her.

30

THE FOOTBRIDGE SHATTERED INTO THE
creek below, and Sophia shattered with it.

Pain shocked through her legs, her arms. The creek
only contained a burble of water—it was mostly stones.
They ground into Sophia's skin.

She lay there, stunned.

When she first heard someone call her name, she
thought it was just a trick of her imagination. Then the
voice came again: "Sophia! Is that you?"

Lacey Wilkens ran to the creek bank and peered
down at her. Another girl joined her, then another. They
were on bikes too.

"Are you okay?" one of them squeaked.

Lacey clambered down into the creek and helped Sophia out from beneath her bike. There were shards of wood everywhere. Lacey picked pieces of it from Sophia's hair.

"What happened?" she demanded.

Sophia was still dizzy from it all. "Everything's falling," she mumbled. "The bookcase, and now the bridge—"

"The bookcase? What bookcase?"

Sophia shook her head and tried to pull herself together. The fall wasn't as far as it had felt at the time. She was fine. No broken bones. Nothing irreparably damaged. There was no need to freak out.

"The bridge collapsed," she said.

"Yeah," Lacey said. She laughed. "I can see that. You were going super fast."

Sophia shook out the aches in her legs. Her elbows and shins were bleeding a little, but not much. The bike—well, hopefully the bike was all right.

"What were you in such a big rush for?" Lacey asked. "Are you still sick? You weren't at school."

"Oh. I—" Sophia racked her brain for something to say, but all excuses had fled. It didn't help that Lacey's friends—were they Sophia's friends too?—kept staring at them from the bank. "I'm going to see my dad."

Lacey's nose wrinkled. She flashed Sophia a knife-sharp smile and rolled her eyes. "I thought you only had to see him on weekends now. Isn't he breaking the law or something, making you see him during the week?"

A hot flush rose in Sophia's cheeks. "I *want* to see him," she snapped. "And it's none of your business."

Lacey gaped at her. Her hands went very tight at her sides. "I don't know what's wrong with you right now," she hissed. She swallowed hard, and Sophia felt a pang of regret. "You agreed with me a couple days ago."

She didn't wait for Sophia to reply, just scrambled back up the bank and muttered something that might have been *See you at school.* She hopped on her bike and sped off. The other girls followed suit.

Alone again, Sophia lugged her bike out of the creek. She shouldn't have talked to Lacey like that. Not when the other girl had just been so nice.

But why would one of her friends be so rude about her father?

Still, Lacey had seemed honestly shocked by Sophia's reaction. Which meant she was probably telling the truth when she said that Sophia had been complaining about her father just a few days ago.

Sophia couldn't imagine doing something like that. She couldn't imagine saying a single bad thing about her father to DJ, let alone to Lacey Wilkens. No matter how strong their friendship was in this world.

But maybe that was the problem. At the end of the day, Sophia wasn't the Sophia who'd been here in this world last week. Maybe *she* wouldn't have said those things, but that didn't mean Other Sophia wouldn't have.

And now Sophia had taken her place.

The thought shook her even more than it had that morning, or the night before. She started biking again and was halfway home before she realized she was going in the wrong direction. By then it was too late. She didn't feel like turning around again.

The blue car was in the driveway again, and her mom's voice rang out when Sophia came in.

"Sophie? Where did you go?"

"Nowhere," Sophia said.

She rushed through the house until she found her mother, until she could wrap her arms around her and try to forget everything else.

31

THAT NIGHT SOPHIA DREAMED SHE WAS back in her old world. When she woke the next morning, she spent several minutes lying confused in bed, the alarm clock buzzing on her nightstand.

Was she still dreaming? Which bed, in which world, was she lying in?

In a minute, who would come to her bedroom door, stick their head in, and say, *Sophia, aren't you getting up?*

The alarm clock kept buzzing. Sophia closed her eyes and tried to sort herself out.

"Sophie? Honey, it's time to get up."

Sophia felt a pang in her chest she couldn't understand. Relief and dread and yearning and fear, all at once.

"Sophie?" Her mom came in just as Sophia opened her eyes again. "You awake?"

"I'm awake," Sophia said, so softly that the alarm clock buried her voice. She forced herself up so she could shut it off.

Her mom sat on the edge of her bed. "You feeling sick again?"

Sophia shook her head. Her mom studied her a moment longer, and Sophia tried to smile. "All right," she said. "Up you go, then. Don't want to be late."

Breakfast helped settle her stomach and ease the warring feelings in her chest. It was easy to be distracted from everything else when her mom was around.

Everything would work out. Would be okay.

"Just a couple more days, right, Sophie?" her mom said as she dug for her keys.

"Hmm?" Sophia still didn't know how she felt about being called *Sophie*. It should have been nice. There was nothing wrong with *Sophie*, and everything nice about her mother being here, alive and healthy and able to give her nicknames.

And yet.

It wasn't bad. Just strange.

"A couple more days until what?" she asked.

"You didn't forget, did you?" her mother said teasingly. "You've been talking about this for ages—the solar eclipse on Sunday."

Sophia went very still.

"Wasn't that—" she started to say, then clamped her mouth shut.

So many other things had shifted around, changed. Who was to say that the solar eclipse wasn't one of them?

"Sophie?" Her mom paused at the door, looking concerned.

"Yeah," Sophia whispered. "I'm excited."

Sophia missed DJ every step of the way to school. Ever since that first time they'd run into each other, he'd met up with her as frequently as he could so they could walk together. It wasn't a terribly long walk, and often they'd spent all of it talking about past Memories. But sometimes they'd talked about other things too—books and TV shows and the places they wished they could visit.

We can still be friends, Sophia told herself. There was nothing keeping her from going up to him at school and starting a conversation. But would they still be able to talk about the same things? Did this version of DJ still love to draw, and aspire to attend a magnet high school, and dream about Paris?

And what about the friends the Sophia of this world already had? Would Lacey forgive her after what had happened yesterday? Did Sophia even want to be friends with her, after what Lacey had said about her dad?

Apparently, Other Sophia would have been fine with it. Did that mean Sophia should be as well?

Her head was so full of thoughts that they dragged down her feet. She barely got to school before the warning bell rang, and she was halfway to Ms. Mallory's classroom, where she usually had first-period pre-algebra, when she realized it might not be her classroom anymore.

She peeked through the doorway, trying to see if her usual seat was taken.

"What're you doing here?" Lacey said from the second row.

Sophia hesitated. "This isn't my first-period class?"

"I'm not trying to be rude," Lacey said, "but I think you need to get your head checked out, Sophia. You've been . . . off."

She didn't sound malicious about it, but she didn't sound like she particularly liked this new version of Sophia either.

"Yeah," Sophia said quietly. "I know."

Lacey studied her a moment longer, her arms folded against her stomach. Then she sighed. "You have Ms. Dall for science, remember?"

"Right," Sophia said, as if she did remember. She was pretty sure Lacey didn't believe her, but she didn't stick around to find out.

She had no idea where Ms. Dall's classroom was, or who Ms. Dall was, but all the seventh-grade classrooms were in the same wing of the school. She moved from room to room, checking the names outside.

She slowed as she approached Mr. Rae's classroom. He hadn't closed his door yet, and his big, booming voice echoed into the hall.

He still had the LEARN AROUND TOWN bulletin board up outside his classroom. It was even decorated the same, filled with articles about the upcoming solar eclipse. Sophia couldn't stop staring at it, drinking in the familiarity.

It was hard to believe that the eclipse hadn't happened

yet in this world. She'd be able to see it properly this time, maybe even get her hands on a pair of those special sun-viewing glasses. She'd stare as the moon covered up the sun, and when it was over, she'd head back inside and eat dinner with her mother.

She'd have dinner with her again the next day, and the one after that, and the one after that. She had decades of dinners to look forward to. Decades of new memories to make. Her mom at high school graduation. Her mom waving her off to college. Her mom teaching her all the stuff moms were supposed to teach their kids.

Sophia frowned as she reached the bottom of Mr. Rae's display. He'd added something new under the poster advertising the eclipse model at the library. It wasn't much, just a flyer stating the place and time for a symposium downtown.

THE UNIVERSES, THIS ONE AND BEYOND, it said. Sophia's eyes caught on the photo of the speaker. A familiar man looked out at her from behind horn-rimmed glasses.

RENOWNED ASTROPHYSICIST, boasted the flyer.

NICOLAS SCOT, PHD.

32

SOPHIA'S DAD PULLED UP TO THE HOUSE at exactly ten fifteen a.m. Saturday morning. He drove the same truck he'd always driven, wore the same combination of faded blue jeans and printed T-shirt he'd always favored, and only looked Sophia's mom in the eye half the time as they said hello.

Not that Sophia's mom noticed, because she was doing the same thing.

"Have fun!" she said as Sophia got in the truck, but the notes in her voice were all strange, like a song played in the wrong key.

When Sophia's dad had called last night to ask what she wanted to do today, he'd sounded surprised that a symposium at a college downtown was her top choice, but he'd agreed to take her.

Any particular reason? he'd asked.

Sophia had mumbled something about how cool the eclipse was, and how it had gotten her excited about science and physics and stuff. But to be honest, she wasn't sure herself.

She'd initially searched for Mr. Scot because he might understand what she was going through, as a crosser of universes. But now that she'd thought more about it, there was no reason he'd know who she was in this world. No reason he'd want to speak to some random kid who showed up at his symposium.

Besides, what would they talk about? Sophia had done it. She'd crossed.

Still. This might be her only chance to speak with this Mr. Scot. She should take it, just in case.

"You have a good week at school?" her dad asked as they merged onto the highway.

"School's fine," Sophia said.

He nodded. It was a few more seconds before he asked her another question—about Lacey this time, and whether they had plans for summer break. Sophia had no idea if they did or not, so she sidestepped the question. Her dad didn't seem to mind. In fact, he seemed to expect her mumbled response.

"How's work?" Sophia ventured.

The question surprised her dad so much that he turned to stare at her—and nearly swerved into the next lane. Sophia shouted. He yanked the car back into its proper place.

"How's work?" he echoed, as if he didn't understand the words. He laughed and pushed his hair out of his face. "Work's good, I guess. Why?"

Sophia shrugged. "Anything interesting happen?"

Back in her old world, her dad often told her stories about the people he'd encountered that day at Tom's. Sometimes, though less often, he had stories from the law office too.

Most of the lawyers were gone by the time he showed up to clean, but the late-night phone calls he overheard were some of the most interesting. He and Sophia would piece together stories about million-dollar divorce settlements and scandalous lawsuits, making the details more and more ridiculous until they couldn't breathe for laughing.

Apparently the Sophia of this world didn't do that sort of thing with her dad, because he just said, "Uh, well, Lacey's big brother came into Tom's last night."

"Oh," Sophia said in relief, "you still work at Tom's."

"You feeling okay, Sophia?" He laughed, but the question didn't feel entirely like a joke.

"Never mind," she said quickly. "Lacey's brother came in, and then what?"

Her dad launched into a story that involved Lacey's brother, half the high school football team, and twenty pounds of hamburger. By the time they reached the campus, they were both laughing.

Sophia could almost pretend that this was just another Saturday back home, with her dad having a good day and the two of them setting out for an adventure.

That all disappeared when she saw the poster for Mr. Scot's—*Dr. Scot's*—talk. She took a deep breath.

Inside, crowds of people clustered in an atrium, most of them carrying plates of fancy crackers and vegetable dip. The older people wore crisp button-downs or solemn sheath dresses. The younger ones—the college students—were more casually dressed, but Sophia's dad still looked vaguely uncomfortable as they passed through the crowd.

Sophia let him shepherd her into the auditorium, out of sight of the others. They picked seats toward the back. She waited long enough for it not to seem suspicious, then told her dad she needed to find a bathroom.

She slipped out the door in search of Mr. Scot.

It took a few minutes, but she found him off to the side, chatting with a much older man in a gray suit. Sophia weaved her way toward them, was just about to interrupt when someone else got there first: a lovely woman with long black curls.

"Ah," Mr. Scot said, smiling. "Frank, this is my wife, Gloria. Gloria, this is Frank—he's a professor here."

The cellist—Sophia knew it was her, felt it in her bones—shook Frank's hand and said she was pleased to meet him.

"Mr. Scot," Sophia said. Then, louder, "Dr. Scot!"

The adults stopped talking. All three bore variations of the same look on their faces: confusion, mild amusement.

"Yes?" said Dr. Scot. Sophia marveled at the easy smile on his face, the openness in his eyes.

"Can I talk with you?" she said.

He laughed, and the others laughed with him. Sophia

bit her lip to keep from saying something rude.

"Of course," Dr. Scot said. "What about?"

Sophia didn't need to look to know that Gloria and Frank were still staring at her. "Can we talk alone?"

Dr. Scot hesitated, checking his watch.

"They want you in there in ten minutes, dear," Gloria said.

"Right, right," Dr. Scot said. He glanced around, then gestured to a corner of the atrium near the water fountains. It wasn't exactly private, but it was away from the others. "How about we go talk over there . . . ?"

He paused, waiting for her to fill in her name.

"Sophia," Sophia said.

She watched him carefully. She knew not to expect any kind of recognition, but she couldn't help hoping for one anyway. There was none.

"Sophia," he said with a smile, and waited for her to lead the way.

Sophia knew she had to hurry. But even after they left Gloria and Frank behind, she couldn't find the words she needed to say.

She cleared her throat. "Your research is pretty cool."

"Why thank you," he said. "I'm lucky to work on

such an interesting topic. Looking into parallel universes started out as just a side project, and—"

"Looking," Sophia said, latching onto the word. "Do you think that's possible? To look into parallel universes?"

She knew by the way he laughed that the answer was no. "I mean, I look into various theories about parallel universes. Do you know what a Hubble volume is?"

Sophia shook her head.

"How about wave function collapse? The many-worlds interpretation? Okay, how about the Big Bang?" He smiled when she nodded. "And inflation?"

"Like for money?"

"No, no—*inflation*." He made an expanding gesture with his hands, miming something getting larger.

"Like a balloon."

"But instead of a balloon, it's the universe. The idea is that right after the Big Bang, the universe went through an extremely brief period of accelerated expansion." His hands zoomed apart. "But then it slowed down. Only, it's theorized that there are some pockets of the universe that are still accelerating and could be . . . ballooning out into other universes, which, in turn, could bud out other universes, and so on, and so on."

Sophia let him go on for a little longer, then interrupted. "What about crossing? What does your research say about people crossing into other universes?"

"Not much. It's a bit beyond the scope of my research, anyway. I'm sure there are people theorizing about it—well, I know there are people theorizing about it, but . . ." He waved a hand. "It's fringe science, you know."

"But say someone did cross," Sophia said. "What would happen?"

He shifted, uncomfortable under the fierceness of her questioning. "That's not possible to say for sure. I won't say crossing itself is impossible. Who knows what we might discover in years to come? But I can't imagine universes would take well to . . . foreign intrusion."

"Foreign intrusion?"

"It's like . . ." He thought for a moment. "You know how when someone gets an organ transplant, they need to take medicine to keep their body from rejecting the new organ?"

Sophia nodded.

"Well, I imagine it might be the same way with universes. Your heart might look roughly the same as the heart of another girl your size and age, but it's not. Not as far as your body is concerned. Your heart has all sorts of factors that make it unique to you. If doctors took another girl's heart and put it inside you, your body wouldn't be thrilled about it. It would send your immune system to attack it, get rid of this new foreign entity."

A cold shiver passed through Sophia's body. She remembered, suddenly, the way the footbridge had collapsed on her yesterday. She'd written it off as an unfortunate accident.

Had it been something more?

"You're saying the universe would try to . . . kill me off? I mean, if I were a crosser."

"Perhaps." Dr. Scot was getting more excited about the topic. "Or I suppose it might try to bend the other way. Change *itself* to try to match the intruder."

Change itself? But if this world changed itself to match Sophia's old world . . .

What would that mean for her mother?

"I—" she said, but didn't get any further. The man in the gray suit—Frank—waved at them before gesturing toward the auditorium doors.

"I'm sorry," Dr. Scot said. "I'm afraid I have to go. Will you be around after the talk? We can continue our discussion then."

"Yeah," Sophia said quietly. "Sure."

But she wasn't sure she would be.

33

SOPHIA MADE IT THROUGH HALF OF
Dr. Scot's presentation before she tapped her dad on the
arm and whispered, "Can we go?"

"You sure?" her dad whispered back.

Sophia nodded. It was hard to understand Dr. Scot's
lecture, to tease meaning from the charts and figures he
kept projecting onto the screen.

Maybe she would've had more luck if she could stop
thinking about their earlier conversation. About the con-
sequences of crossing.

They snuck out the back of the auditorium, left the
car in the parking lot, and went to get ice cream. Ice

cream led to a walk through campus, and lunch at a hole-in-the-wall Vietnamese place, the two of them lapsing in and out of conversation.

All the while, Sophia chatted and laughed and tried to bury the thoughts roiling inside her. It was impossible.

Had she come all this way for nothing? Done all this just for the universe to kick her out again?

"What next?" her dad asked as they wandered back toward the car. "You want to catch a movie?"

Sophia turned so she was walking backward, balancing on the edge of the curb. "Maybe. What's playing?"

"There's that one with the space whale," her dad said. Sophia giggled and made a face. "What? I swear that's what it's about. I've seen the trailers—there's a whale, and it's definitely in space. I'm sure—"

Sophia never did get to hear what it was her dad was sure about.

Because at that exact moment, the car hit her.

One second, she was walking heel to toe on the curb, her arms out for balance.

The next, she was flat against the asphalt. The world spun. People kept screaming.

"Sophia!" Her dad threw himself down next to her,

pressed her down when she tried to get up. "Stay still. You all right?"

He gripped her shoulder so hard it hurt—everything hurt.

People pressed around them, a claustrophobic ring that made it hard for Sophia to breathe. Someone shouted for someone else to jot down a license number. The driver had slammed on the brakes before hitting Sophia, then swerved and zoomed off again.

She tried to talk but couldn't. Her dad said something, but he sounded weirdly far away. He leaned closer, and suddenly she was off the street, was being carried to a bench.

Breath returned to Sophia's lungs. She gulped in air, trying to make up for lost time.

"I'm okay," she said. "I'm okay. I'm okay."

Her father sat her down and made her wriggle her ankles and kick out her legs, before moving upward and getting her to do the same with her elbows and wrists.

Sophia humored him until he was satisfied, and shook her head when he asked if she was dizzy, if her head hurt, if she'd hit it against the ground when she fell.

"Someone's already called 911," a woman told them. "The police will be here soon."

Sophia's dad thanked her distractedly. "You're absolutely sure you're okay?" he asked.

She nodded. She didn't want to think about how this was the second accident she'd had in two days. The second thing that could have killed or seriously harmed her.

"Can we go home?" she said quietly.

"Yeah, yeah," he said, "of course. Maybe to the hospital first. And we have to wait for the police—" He cut himself off. "You mean back home with your mom?"

"You could come too," Sophia said.

He hesitated, then shook his head. "I don't think so, Sophia."

"Please?" she begged. "Please, just this once? I won't ask again. Just this one time."

Maybe it was the desperation in her voice. Maybe it was how she'd almost gotten flattened by a car. Or maybe it was something else entirely.

But finally, her dad nodded.

"If your mom agrees," he said.

Sophia's dad called her mom during the drive home to fill her in, which meant she was pacing outside the house by the time they arrived. She rushed up to Sophia as soon as she stepped down from the truck, inspecting her for scrapes and bruises.

"You okay?" she demanded, and looked to Sophia's dad for confirmation when Sophia nodded.

"Can Dad stay for dinner?" Sophia asked.

Her mom's eyes darted back to her. She hesitated in a way that suggested the answer might be no, and Sophia's dad looked uncomfortable enough to bow out of the situation altogether.

"Please?" Sophia said. She tried her hardest to look like someone who'd very nearly gotten run over by a car an hour ago.

"Go inside, sweetheart," her mom said. "We'll be there in a minute."

The use of the word *we* was encouraging, at least. Sophia nodded and headed in.

Maybe it was wrong of her to force this evening together. Maybe this was yet another thing that Other Sophia would never have done, because she knew all the nuances that had forced her parents apart, had set them down the roads leading to this particular end.

But Sophia wasn't that Sophia. And she wanted, just once, to have dinner with both her parents again.

A few minutes later, her mom and dad came to find her in the living room. She'd perched on the couch, pretending to watch TV.

"All right," her mom said. "What do you want to eat?"

It was too early to be talking about dinner, but Sophia didn't want to mess anything up. She blurted out the first thing that came to mind: "Piperade."

"Piperade?" said her parents in unison.

"It's peppers and tomatoes and onions and stuff," Sophia said. "Don't worry. I'll look up a recipe."

Luckily, they had most of the ingredients on hand. Her parents worked quietly next to each other, chopping onions and slicing peppers. The kitchen was tiny, but they never touched. There was a rhythm to the way they avoided each other, guessing the way the other moved before they did it.

They ate while the sun was still high above the horizon. Sophia's mom sat on one side of her, her dad on the other. They talked about nothing in particular, and laughed at all of Sophia's jokes.

Afterward, while her dad started the dishes and her mom scooped out bowls of ice cream, Sophia lingered at the kitchen counter, her chin resting in her cupped hands, and soaked in everything she could. Burned this moment into her mind. The whisper of her mother's shoes against the floor. The fullness of the kitchen when it was filled with three bodies. The way her father snuck a bite of ice cream while he loaded the dishwasher, and her mother laughed in surprise when she caught him.

Whatever rift had formed between them these past few years, maybe it would heal again. Or maybe the wounds were already too deep, and things would never be the same. Sophia knew which one she hoped for.

But she also knew she couldn't stay to find out.

She'd been here less than a week, and the universe had tried to kill her twice. How many more near misses with cars, trains, rabid dogs, and slipping kitchen knives would there be if she stayed longer?

Even if she managed to stay alive, what if the universe came after her mother next, the way Dr. Scot had theorized?

Her mother was vibrant, healthy—so, so alive in this world.

And once Sophia left, another version of Sophia would replace her. The one who belonged here.

The one who hadn't lost her mother six years ago

and been forced to cope in her own broken way.

Her chest ached. A low, steady pain that pressed like a rock at her ribs.

"What're you thinking so hard about, Sophie?" her mother teased. She bumped Sophia's hip gently as she passed, carrying the bowls of ice cream.

The solar eclipse would come tomorrow here. That was so little time. Why couldn't it have come in a month, or a year?

She wanted more time. She needed more time.

"Your ice cream is going to melt, Sophia," her dad said from the table.

"Or your father's going to eat it," her mom warned.

She needed more time.

But this—this right here—was all she was going to get.

It wasn't enough.

But it was something.

"Coming," Sophia said, and joined them at the table.

34

MORNING CAME TOO QUICKLY. SOPHIA woke far earlier than she usually did. For the first hour, she just lay in bed, thinking.

About her father.

About her conversation with Lacey and the other girls.

About DJ.

About Luke.

About the Sophie of this world and the Sophia she really was.

She squeezed her eyes shut as tightly as she could and thought about her mother. The one who'd died, and the one who lay sleeping down the hall.

Who Sophia could wake right now, if she wanted to.

Who she'd never have seen like this, if she hadn't come to this world.

Who she'd never see again, when she went back to her old one.

When the thinking got to be too much, she got up and roamed the house, pattering through all the rooms on bare feet. Whispering good-bye to the life that might have been hers, if things had gone differently.

She reached her mother's room last.

The door was closed. She pressed her hand against it, almost pushed it open. At the last moment, she changed her mind.

She went downstairs and made breakfast, and waited for her mother to wake.

By the time her mother came downstairs, the sun was high in the sky, and the strange, dreamy mood of dawn had broken. It felt like any normal morning.

"You want tacos tonight?" she asked, pecking Sophia on the forehead as she poured herself more cereal. "Or we can make spaghetti again."

"Either's okay," Sophia said.

"Tacos it is, then." Her mom took out the meat to defrost, then went looking for her keys. Sophia had a whisper of a memory—a real memory, faint but warm—of her mother always looking for her keys.

If she stayed, how much more would she remember about her mother? How much more would she learn?

But she couldn't stay.

"Solar eclipse today!" her mom said, flashing her a smile. "Are you going to go see it with Lacey? I'm going to step outside too, if I can. Let's compare notes tonight?"

Sophia bit back the urge to ask her to stay home. To say that she wasn't feeling well again, that they needed to lounge around the house and eat pancakes and watch the solar eclipse from their driveway.

"Okay," she said instead.

Her mom cheered quietly as she found her keys beneath a pile of mail.

"See you later," she said, and made a startled noise when Sophia darted from the table and crushed her in a hug. She laughed. "Everything okay?"

"I love you," Sophia said. "I love you. *I love you.*"

"I love you too, Sophie," her mom said. "Honey, is something wrong?"

Sophia shook her head. Stayed buried in her mother's arms for as long as she could.

And then, after—after her mom had disentangled herself and asked if Sophia was sure she was all right, and Sophia had nodded—after her mom had hugged her and went to pull on her shoes—after she'd gone out the door and climbed into her car—after she'd honked merrily at Sophia as she drove off—Sophia stared after her, watching.

Trying to commit everything to memory.

To never forget.

Eventually, she had to turn away. There were still traces of her father in the house. Sophia found a forgotten sock in the dresser, a pile of winter clothing stuffed in the back of a closet. A man's razor rattled around the bathroom drawer.

She could have grabbed any of it to be her anchor for her trip home. But none of it felt right. In fact, most of it felt silly. She knew her father. She carried so much of him inside her—how could it be helped by a sock or a razor?

There was nowhere to get things to tie her to DJ

and Luke, either. Sophia had to hope that her memories would be enough.

She waited until the right time, then headed for Donway Shallows, picking her way through the beer cans and broken glass until she stood exactly where she'd stood four days ago, in another world.

She squeezed her hands into fists, then let them relax again.

She took a deep breath and closed her eyes as the sun began to fade.

A chill struck her. Gave her a full-body shudder.

Home, she pleaded.

Take me home.

35

OPENING HER EYES WAS LIKE WAKING FROM a dream. Sunlight seeped through the mill, faint at first, but growing.

DJ stood on her left, Luke on her right. They held hands, the three of them forming a silent, awed circle. None of them spoke.

Bit by bit, the sun crept from behind the moon. The world grew bright enough for Sophia to see the freckles on Luke's nose, the curve of DJ's mouth.

She squeezed their hands. DJ's mouth quirked upward, along with an eyebrow, and that was enough to make her laugh—laugh without knowing why she was laughing. He started laughing too, the two of them lost in fits of giggles as Luke scowled and snapped, "What? What? Nothing's that funny."

Sophia dissolved into another peal of laughter.

Maybe there were infinite other worlds out there, infinite other parallel universes, in which she hadn't decided to come back. Or DJ hadn't. Or Luke hadn't. Maybe in other universes right now, she was standing here all alone.

She was so, so glad she wasn't in any of them.

There was so much to talk about—to ask about what each of them had seen in the worlds they'd visited.

"How was—" DJ and Sophia said at the same time, before cutting themselves off and laughing embarrassedly.

"You first," Sophia said. "How was your stepdad?"

"Wonderful," DJ said, and sounded like he meant it, one hundred percent. "And your mom?"

"Just like I remembered," Sophia said softly. She turned to Luke and smiled. "How was life with Marni?"

"Annoying," he grumbled, but didn't sound like he meant it at all.

For now, they left it at that. They didn't press for

details. Didn't ask how and why they'd made the decision to return. Just walked together in contemplative silence. The boys had faraway looks in their eyes, as if they were still peeking into parallel worlds.

Sophia wondered if she and DJ would still have their Memories. Maybe crossing over and coming back again had shifted something—in them or in the world. Maybe the Memories were gone.

It was a sorrowful thought, but not an unbearable one. Even if Sophia got no more new Memories, she'd keep the ones she already had. The normal memories too.

And, of course, she'd have that cherished dinner she'd shared with both her parents. The piperade and the ice cream afterward, butter pecan.

Jessup Middle sat deserted in the midday sun, all the kids already hustled back indoors.

"I'm not even supposed to be at school," Luke mumbled, but made no move to leave as the three of them reached the back lot.

DJ winced. "How much trouble you think we're going to be in?"

"Maybe they haven't noticed," Sophia said. "Maybe

the solar eclipse will smooth things over. It'll just be like . . . a blip."

But it wasn't to be. The first teacher to see them—Ms. Renalds, Sophia's math teacher—freaked out and dragged them to the front office, making chiding noises the whole way.

The three of them stayed silent. At least until they arrived at the office, where Luke's parents huddled anxiously on folding chairs, and DJ's mother interrogated someone—Nicole, probably—on the phone, and Sophia's dad—

"Sophia!" he shouted. He looked relieved and worried and angry, all at once. "Sophia—"

Sophia didn't hear the rest of his sentence. Everyone else in the office had snapped to attention at the sound of her name, and now they were all talking too, barreling toward the kids. A rush of noise and feeling.

Sophia gripped onto her dad, held on as tightly as she could.

Sophia's dad sighed yet again as he climbed into the driver's seat of his truck. Sophia sat buckled in on the passenger's side. She'd been listening to him sigh ever since he calmed down from his initial wave of questions—the same questions everyone else had been asking: *Are you okay? Where did you go? Why did you go? Weren't you thinking? Whose idea was this?*

Sophia had shrugged and mumbled her way through them all, answering the questions that needed answers, ignoring the ones that were obviously rhetorical. She and the boys had already decided on their story before getting back to school. To anyone who asked, they'd left school because they'd gotten bored waiting for the eclipse and had gone to find something more interesting to do. They'd headed back once they realized they'd been away too long.

It wasn't a great story, and an even worse excuse, but it served its purpose.

Eventually, her dad had given up on questioning her and told the administrators he was taking Sophia home. That was when the sighing had started.

Bye, Sophia had told DJ and Luke silently. They nodded at her. DJ gave her a faint smile when his mother wasn't watching.

The truck engine rumbled as it warmed up. Sophia's dad fussed with his seat belt, then released it again and turned to Sophia like he wanted to say something. Nothing came.

He shook his head and turned back to his seat belt.

Sophia expected that to be that. Expected a silent ride back home. To a quiet afternoon, where they'd talk about everything but what had happened, ignoring it until it sank beneath the weight of passing days.

Instead her father said quietly, "I thought you'd run away. I was really scared when they called and said you'd disappeared."

Sophia stared at her hands. Her father had never told her that he was scared before. She didn't know how to respond.

To her surprise, she didn't need to. Her dad kept talking. "I should have gone up to talk to you last night. I was going to do it this morning, but something came up at Tom's, and I had to go in early. I didn't want to wake you."

"Oh," Sophia said. She shrugged and didn't look up. "That's okay."

Her father clicked on his seat belt. He'd gotten the truck halfway out of their parking space when Sophia said, suddenly, "I don't want to move."

Her voice cut through the silence. Her dad pumped the brakes. The tires squealed. They both lurched forward.

"Sorry," Sophia mumbled, after they'd both caught their breaths.

Her dad shifted the truck back into park.

"What?" he said quietly.

Sophia didn't meet his eyes.

"Sophia?"

"I don't want to move," she said. "I don't—I don't think we should move. I like it here. I like our house, and I have friends here, and I want to keep going to school here, and I don't think things would be better if we went anywhere else, okay? I just don't."

Her dad was quiet. Sophia peeked up at him, took in the startled look on his face as it slowly morphed into something softer.

"You're really worried about this, huh?" he said.

Sophia caught herself half shrug and nodded instead.

"I wasn't thinking all that seriously about moving, Sophia. I was just frustrated with the town yesterday, and it was a thought that came up. I guess we misunderstood each other, huh?"

Sophia nodded again.

"I would talk with you before making any kind of decision like that," he said. "I promise, okay? And—and about other things too. I want us to talk about things, Sophia. All right?"

"All right," Sophia said.

"No more running away," he said. "For both of us."

She smiled, just a little bit.

Her dad started backing out of the parking space again. This time, he got as far as the edge of the parking lot before he stepped on the brakes again.

"Sophia?"

"Yeah?" she said.

He smiled. Set his palm atop her head the way he had when she'd been younger. It seemed to take him a long moment to decide what he was going to say—or maybe just how to say it. "Thanks, Sophia."

"For what?"

"For being you."

EPILOGUE

THE CEMETERY WHERE SOPHIA'S MOTHER and Luke's sister were buried wasn't a large one. Their town was too small for large cemeteries. The dead, like the living, spent their days nestled close among the same families and neighbors and friends and enemies they'd known since forever.

Luke brought flowers: red and yellow dahlias with their layers upon layers of tiny petals. Sophia didn't bring flowers, because that was never the way she and her father had done it. They brought her mother things like peppermint candies, or plastic toys won from roadside carnivals. Things more permanent, her father said, than flowers.

Today she carried in her pocket a little doodle she'd made. DJ was teaching her how to draw—or trying to teach her, anyway. Sophia wasn't sure she *was* teachable. The doodle, which was supposed to be her father, bore only the faintest resemblance.

Actually, it didn't bear any resemblance to her father at all. But Sophia figured her mother would understand.

Luke split wordlessly away when they neared his sister's grave. Sophia continued onward. DJ came with her, though he lagged behind when she stopped in front of her mother's headstone.

"Hi," Sophia said quietly to her mother.

She knelt and unfolded the doodle. Sometimes when she'd come in the past, she'd chatted a bit with her mom. But she felt awkward doing that with DJ there, even if he was hanging back to give her space.

She found a pretty rock to put on top of the doodle, so the wind wouldn't blow it away. Then she ran her hand over the sun-warmed tombstone and stood.

"Let's go find Luke," she said.

His sister's grave lay in a dip of the land by a magnolia tree. Sophia's mom lay in a plot by herself—her family lived several states away now—but Marni McPherson lay surrounded by a swath of grandparents and great-uncles and aunts.

Luke had already laid his bouquet of flowers by her tombstone. His head was bowed, but he looked up when Sophia and DJ got closer.

Sophia thought he might have been crying. With someone else, she might have reached out to him. Hugged him, maybe. Tried to repeat all the meaningless comfort words that people said when others were grieving and there was nothing actually helpful to say.

But she was pretty sure Luke wanted none of those things. It wasn't his way.

For her part, she had no tears today. Which wasn't to say she wasn't sad, the way she was always sad when she came to her mother's grave—the way she was always, and would always, be sad when she thought about her, and missed her. But it wasn't the sort of sadness that incited tears.

Grief, Sophia thought, was a funny thing.

A horrible thing, she wanted to add, but after a moment, she wasn't sure if that was right. She wasn't sure if grief could be called a good or bad thing—it simply *was*.

It was what happened when you loved someone, and

then you lost them. And the loving someone part—that was good. And the losing them part—that was awful.

But the grief—the grief was just waves in the ocean, or the ache in your hands after you'd stuck them in the snow.

An aftereffect. A consequence.

It only felt right to visit Mr. Scot together, but actually finding the time took a while. Sophia wasn't sure about the boys, but she'd gained a new appreciation for just being at home, enjoying her house being the house she'd always known. Besides, her father was keeping closer tabs on her too.

So by the time the three of them set out to Mr. Scot's together, it was a week until summer break. They headed over after swimming in Luke's neighborhood pool, Sophia's hair dripping down her shirt the whole way.

Mr. Scot's house came into view, dark blue and gray-doored. Sophia knocked firmly on the door. Luke shuffled along the line of bushes standing sentinel in front of the house, calling for Schrödinger.

"Do you want to come to dinner?" DJ said suddenly, as they waited for Mr. Scot to answer. "You and your dad

I mean, you can come by yourself, too. But my mom, she told me to ask if you and your dad wanted to come have dinner."

He cleared his throat.

"Oh, um," Sophia said. She didn't remember the last time she and her dad had gone to anyone's house for dinner. "Yeah, okay."

"Okay," DJ said, sounding relieved.

She smiled at him, and he smiled back.

"I can't find Schrödinger," Luke complained.

"He's probably inside," DJ said, and knocked again at the door.

They waited a bit longer, but still, no one came.

Luke lost patience and start peeking into windows. He ran from one window to another, cupping his hands around his face to get a better view.

Sophia knocked harder this time—and jumped as the door popped open. She and DJ exchanged a look.

"Luke!" Sophia shouted. "Luke, come here!"

She eased the door open wider and stepped inside.

"Mr. Scot?" DJ called as he followed behind her. "Your door was open."

No reply.

Luke rushed to join them in the darkened foyer. "No Schrödinger," he said, as if nothing else mattered, and loped down the hall in search of him.

Sophia and DJ checked the study first. It sat untouched, all the knickknacks and old books lumped in dusty piles, all the papers and newspaper clippings still pinned to the corkboard. The ancient, sloping armchair still had a dent in the cushion, as if Mr. Scot had been sitting there only moments before. But Sophia didn't think that was true.

She had a suspicion about where Mr. Scot had gone, and if she was right, he must have left quite a while ago.

She left DJ, still rummaging around in the library, and found her way to Mr. Scot's living room. He hadn't even tried to clean up the collapsed bookcase. Everything lay where it had fallen.

Sophia rustled around in the debris until she found what she was looking for: the glass-blown bowl, and resin, and lipstick.

She hadn't realized their significance the last time she'd seen them. She hadn't realized the significance of Mr. Scot's constant injuries, either. The unlikely tilting of the bookcase.

But now she thought she did.

"I found him!" Luke shouted happily. His voice rang through the old house. "I found Schrödinger!"

"What about Mr. Scot?" Sophia heard DJ ask. Luke's reply was too low to comprehend.

But Sophia didn't imagine he'd found any trace of the man. In fact, she didn't think they'd ever find any trace of Mr. Scot ever again—or if they did, it would be a very different Mr. Scot from the one who'd sat in his study and told them about parallel universes.

Don't be disappointed, he'd told Sophia.

He'd learned the same lesson she had about traveling to other worlds. Only he'd learned it much earlier. Maybe he'd even figured out the reason behind his injuries.

If he had, why hadn't he warned her?

Perhaps he'd known that she would have gone anyway. That some things one needed to see for themselves.

"Come on," she called to Luke and DJ, "let's go."

They reconvened on the scraggly front lawn, Luke holding Schrödinger. Sophia smiled. Later she'd tell them her theory about Mr. Scot's whereabouts.

For now—

Well.

"What do you want to do next?" she said.

They had the whole rest of the evening ahead of them, and it was almost summer.

ACKNOWLEDGMENTS

SOPHIA'S STORY HAS LIVED IN MY IMAGI-
nation for a long time, and it has been such a joy to finally
write it. I owe a lot to my agent, Emmanuelle Morgen,
and to my editor, Jennifer Ung, who have championed
this story all the way through. Thank you for all of your
encouragement and hard work!

Thank you to my foreign agent, Whitney Lee, and
to the rest of the team at Aladdin, who have been so
very supportive. *The Memory of Forgotten Things* would
not be the same without you. Special thanks to Jessica
Handelman and Jim Tierney, who crafted such a beautiful cover—I couldn't stop staring at it while revising.

Thank you to my critique partners: Savannah

Foley, Marlowe Brant, and Julie Eshbaugh. You guys are amazing!

Last but not least, thank you to the readers. I hope Sophia's story is as special to you as it is to me.

ABOUT THE AUTHOR

KAT ZHANG LOVES TRAVELING TO PLACES both real and fictional—the former have better souvenirs, but the latter allow for dragons, so it's a tough choice. A graduate of Vanderbilt University, she now spends her free time scribbling poetry, taking photographs, and climbing atop things she shouldn't. You can learn about her travels, literary and otherwise, at katzhangwriter.com.